MOBY
DICK

First published in 2004 by Usborne Publishing Ltd,
Usborne House, 83-85 Saffron Hill,
London EC1N 8RT, England.
www.usborne.com

A catalogue record for this title is available
from the British Library.

UK ISBN 0 7460 6276 1

First published in America 2005
American ISBN 07945 0899 5

Printed in Great Britain

Designed by Brian Voakes
Edited by Jane Chisholm and Rosie Dickins
Cover image of humpback whale © Steve Bloom
Cover design by Neil Francis
Digital manipulation by Nick Wakeford

MOBY DICK

From the story by Herman Melville

Retold by Henry Brook

Illustrated by Bob Harvey

Contents

About Moby Dick

When literary experts argue over which is the greatest novel ever written in English, *Moby Dick* is always a strong contender. It is the story of Captain Ahab's obsessive hunt for the malevolent, snow-white whale, which "dismasted" him on an earlier voyage by tearing off his leg. Ahab's quest for vengeance lies at the heart of the book, but the author, Herman Melville, wanted to do more than write a simple narrative. His book includes discussions, explorations, diversions and descriptions in such numbers and variety they dazzle the reader. *Moby Dick* is a book of books, as mighty and complex as the creature who bears its name.

Melville had already written five novels when he sat down to begin his masterpiece in 1850. He had a solid reputation for creating thrilling sea adventures, but it was the nature and condition of mankind that really fascinated him. His library was full of books on philosophy, religion, science and history, and he was looking for a way to present some of his ideas on these topics to his readers. So, he cast around for a subject that was broad enough to do this. The idea of an attacking whale – nature turning on mankind – set against the backdrop of humans hunting one of the Earth's most majestic creatures to the point of extinction, seemed a perfect choice.

He had heard some tales about a sperm whale sighted in the waters off Chile in the early 1800s that was renowned for two things – it was unusually aggressive, and its skin was as white as pure new wool. Sailors sometimes gave nicknames to notable whales and this animal was known as Mocha Dick, after Mocha, the island where he was first sighted, and Dick, the name of the whaler who had pursued him. Mocha Dick killed several boat crews over the years, until he was fatally harpooned, and his hardiness shocked the whaling community. When his body was examined, no fewer than 20 rusting harpoon heads were found embedded in his blubber. Melville combined this story with another real event – the sinking of the whale ship *Essex* in 1820.

The *Essex* had suffered a fate that made every whaling crew shudder. A rogue sperm whale had rammed her below the waterline repeatedly, as if determined to do her harm. The first mate even recorded the whale's malevolence in his account: "I could distinctly see him smite his jaws together, as if distracted with rage and fury." When the ship sank, the horrified crew drifted for months in small boats. Many of them died of starvation and thirst.

Using elements of this disaster and the story of Mocha Dick, Melville shaped his main character – the white whale, Moby Dick. This destructive, mysterious beast haunts the novel, generating a sense of foreboding that ripples across the pages. Writing and rewriting at a furious pace, Melville created a character worthy of hunting such a beast – Captain Ahab. The captain is an extraordinary individual, teetering between greatness of mind and crazed violent action, after 40 years of scouring the world's oceans for whales. Only the gentle, tender-hearted Ishmael, the book's narrator, has any hope of escaping Ahab's obsessive and hateful influence.

The ship itself, the *Pequod*, carries a selection of the world's races for her crew. As a symbol of human folly, greed and viciousness, the ship has no equal in English literature. Even the name is significant. The Pequod were a "celebrated tribe" of Native American Indians who had been persecuted and hunted out of existence by white settlers.

This reference to the destruction of a people suggests what Melville intended to do with his novel. Some commentators see the *Pequod* as a ship of state, symbolizing a nation with a deranged dictator at the helm. Others see the whaling industry as a wider symbol for the way western societies were dismantling and destroying nature. But, however you approach it, *Moby Dick* is above all a gripping sea adventure, with a range of characters and thrilling scenes that few other books can match.

The Watery Part of the World

Call me Ishmael.

Some years ago, never mind how long precisely, I decided to sail about a bit and see the watery part of the world. This was a habit of mine whenever I noticed the tell-tale signs that I had lingered too long on dry land. These warnings started with sulky moods and fits of bad temper. I might be walking along a street and get the sudden urge to knock a man's hat off his head, for no good reason. I felt irritable and restless at all hours. Soon, a crushing weight of gloomy thoughts overwhelmed me completely, as though a damp and drizzly November day had crept into my heart, and refused to budge. I began to dream of the deep blue sea, yearning for the adventure of exploring distant oceans and barbarous coasts. I was finally enticed back to the crash of the waves like a moth is drawn to the candle flame. Unable to resist any longer, I would get ready to depart.

It might seem strange that I was so in awe of the oceans. But to me they represented all the mysteries of this world we share. When I stared into the sea I caught a glimpse of the infinite universe, its rhythms, patterns and possibilities. Each time, I felt humbled and refreshed by this vision. I sensed the spark of life again, pulsing through my veins.

When I say I was in the habit of going to sea in a ship, I don't mean to say that I boarded as a passenger. To be a passenger you need a wallet, and a wallet isn't much use if you've nothing to put in it – which I never had. Besides, passengers get seasick, they can't sleep in their creaking bunks at night, they argue with each other and complain about their sufferings. So, I didn't board as a passenger, but nor did I travel as a captain or a commodore. All that leadership and responsibility strikes me as a terrible burden; it is all that I can do to take care of myself, without looking after whole navies and ships and their seasick passengers. No, I went to sea as a simple sailor.

There were certain disadvantages to this, I confess. The captain and mates were in the habit of ordering me about, making me hop around in the rigging like a grasshopper in a May meadow. This could wound my pride at first, but I soon got used to it. It didn't make me any less of a man to obey a few orders. It might even have made me a better person. After all, who can say they're not a slave to something, be it a tyrannical captain or some other master? All of us are slaves to our stomachs, aren't we? This shouldn't make us feel bad about ourselves. We all have to take a few knocks in this world. I believe this "universal knock" should be shared around, and all hands should try to soothe each other and be as comfortable as possible.

The advantages of the sailor's life far outweighed the hardships I've described. For example, ship owners made a point of paying me for my trouble, whereas I've never heard of them giving passengers a single penny. Indeed, passengers have to hand over their wallets and buy a ticket. I'd much rather be paid than do the paying. Considering preachers say money is the root of all evil, it's remarkable how many people share my preference. The sailor works and sleeps at the front of the ship, where the air is freshest. But passengers and captains are trapped at the rear of the vessel, and must breathe the atmosphere second hand. I always came back from a voyage fit and healthy, and put this down to the pure air I breathed in as the ship sliced through the surf.

So, I packed my old carpet bag and followed the river down to the sea. The prospect of a new adventure on the oceans made my heart skip, but this time there was an extra reason to be excited. I had decided that on this voyage I wouldn't sail on the merchant vessels I'd chosen before. This time I was going to try my hand at hunting the largest and most powerful creature known to exist – the whale. In my day, this majestic order of animals was hunted for the lamp oil extracted from their blubber. The enormous sperm whale, that clings to the cold, inky depths of the ocean, kept the lights burning in our villages and towns with his oil, and every other part of his body was used for some useful purpose. Most seafaring countries had a special fleet of whale ships and the largest and most prestigious fleet of all sailed out of Nantucket Island, off the coast of Massachusetts. This fine "academy" of whaling was my destination.

I can't quite explain why I had made the choice to hunt the whale. Sometimes we do things without any clear explanation or reason. All I knew was that for months I had been dreaming of the great sea-cruising beasts, and all the far-flung and dangerous corners of the world they wander. These incredible animals roused my curiosity, and the sailors and boats that chased after them were equally mysterious and puzzling. I have always considered it my duty to ponder the riddles of creation and was determined to sign up on a whale ship and investigate that way of life, its pains and pleasures, its strange rituals and customs.

The night before I left, I dreamed of a procession of enormous sperm whales, bubbling and thrashing around my head, gliding in and out of undersea shadows. Chief among them was a great, snow-white phantom of a whale with a crooked jaw. He was prickled all over with bent and rusting harpoons, tangled in trailing ropes and the chipped debris from a thousand smashed boats. As I rubbed my eyes, to get a clearer view of this ghostly sight, he turned and slid into the darkness. The meaning of this dream was lost to me, until much later in my story...

I left Manhattan and arrived in the small port of New Bedford, late on a bitterly cold Saturday night in December. The clipper that sails across to Nantucket had left an hour earlier, and I confess I let out a sigh when I realized I would have to wait in this town until Monday morning. I only had a few coins in my pockets and had hoped to find a boat without delay. New Bedford was a cheerless place, with an Atlantic wind blowing through the streets and long icicles hanging from the buildings.

"Well, Ishmael," I said to myself. "You had better find somewhere to rest your head for the night. And make sure the price is right first."

I trudged along through the snow and frozen mud, until I came to the sign for *The Crossed Harpoons*. Looking in through the doors I could see it was far too plush and tidy for my modest budget. A little further on, I arrived at *The Swordfish Inn*. Pushing my icy nose up to the window pane, I studied the interior. Again, it was too royal for my slender means. Turning from the glow of the fire, and with the tinkle of glasses and laughter ringing in my ears, I moved off into the dark, making for the waterfront. I was looking for "cheap" not "cheerful" – and my instincts told me the inns by the docks would be the most affordable.

The streets were dark as pitch now, save for the occasional candle flickering in a frosty window. I plodded on until I heard a forlorn creaking above my head and, looking up, I saw a dim sign with a painting of a misty fountain upon it.

THE SPOUTER INN
LANDLORD
PETER COFFIN

The building was a tumble-down collection of boards and cracks, trembling in the wind. It had the appearance of hard wear and general poverty. "My kind of place," I muttered to myself, and pushed through the doors.

I found myself in a long room with soot-blackened walls and a ceiling low enough to remind me of the cramped quarters on a ship. Hanging on every wall was an assortment of harpoons, clubs and fearsome spears that sent a shiver down my spine. The only other attempt at decoration was a huge oil painting so filthy and badly lit it looked as though the artist had smeared it with mud. On close inspection I made out a rough shape in the middle of the canvas, the hump of a whale perhaps, and what might have been a flotilla of boats surrounding it, ready to strike with their harpoons. But it was such a boggy, soggy, squiggly picture it was enough to drive a nervous man to distraction. I pushed on into the room.

In one corner I saw two white poles framing a table, but as I approached I realized that the poles were the open jawbones of a whale – so wide you could have driven a stagecoach through the opening. Loitering in the gloom beyond the jaws was a barman, a withered old sailor, who l later discovered went by the name of Jonah, and he sold the guests tumblers of a poison he called ale.

At last I came upon the landlord and managed to inquire about a room.

"I've not one bed free," he told me. "But I might be able to help you. Do you have any objections to sharing the sheets with a harpooner?"

"A harpooner?" I gasped.

"Are you going whaling?" he asked me.

I nodded my head.

"Then you'd best get used to that sort of thing."

I'd never liked sharing a bed with any man. Coffin had obviously never been to sea or he'd have known

17

that sailors are particular about these things and always sleep alone in their hammocks. But the wind outside was raging now, my worn old boots were soaking wet, and I was hungry after walking all day.

"Is he a decent man?" I asked weakly.

"I only have decent men in my inn," the landlord replied with a wink.

"Very well then, I'll take it."

"You won't regret it," he told me with a smile running across his face. "Supper will be ready shortly."

Ten minutes later I was summoned to an adjoining room with five or six other sailors, where a table was laid out for us. The room was unheated – Coffin said he couldn't afford such luxuries – and as cold as Iceland. But the food was roasting hot, and the portions substantial. I dived into a plate of meat and potatoes and a scalding hot mug of tea. When the landlord came in with a plate of dumplings, we all helped ourselves to two or three, except for one sailor who scooped up no less than five.

"You'll give yourself nightmares eating so much," scolded the landlord. I called him over and whispered in his ear, "Is that the harpooner by any chance?"

"Oh no," chortled Coffin. "The harpooner eats nothing but steaks. And he likes them rare."

"So where is he?" I asked, a little nervously.

"He'll be back soon, don't you worry," the landlord answered and he went back to his kitchen smirking.

After dinner, I found a seat in the main room and continued fretting about my mysterious bedfellow. It was getting late now and I couldn't understand what he could be doing out in a storm so violent it was shaking the walls of the inn. When I saw Coffin striding through the room, I waved him over.

"Tell me, Landlord," I asked, "what sort of a chap is this harpooner, that stays out 'till nearly midnight in this foul weather?"

The landlord grinned at my question. "Perhaps he's finding it hard to sell his head," he told me.

"Now listen, Coffin," I said, a rage boiling up in me, "are you telling me this harpooner is trying to sell his own head?"

"Precisely. But the market's saturated."

"With what?" I demanded.

"With heads, of course," Coffin replied with a grin. "Aren't there too many heads in the world?"

"Landlord," I cried. "You and I must understand each other, and rapidly. I demand to know exactly who this harpooner is and whether it's safe to share a bed with him for the night, or if I am in some danger. All this talk of heads is giving me a headache."

"Calm yourself," said Coffin, laying a hand on my shoulder. "This sailor's just back from the South Seas and he brought some embalmed heads with him as curiosities. He's trying to sell them tonight because no one will want to buy them on a Sunday, it being the Sabbath. He tried to go out last Sunday, with four heads on a rope, like a string of onions, and I had to tell him it wasn't a good idea."

At least now I understood the mystery of the heads. But I can't say it made me feel any better about the business. The landlord must have noticed my apprehension.

"Don't worry yourself. It's a huge bed, big enough for two grown men to roll about in without bothering each other. And look at the time, it's already after midnight. He's probably spending the night somewhere else and you'll have the room all to yourself. Now come along with me."

After a moment of nervous deliberation, I followed the landlord up several flights of rickety stairs and into a tiny room at the top of the inn. The bed was pushed up against the far wall and of a fair size, as he had promised. He left me a candle resting on a broken old sea chest that served as the wash stand and dressing table, and wished me goodnight.

I quickly explored the room for any clues I could find about the absent head-seller. There was a heavy bag of clothes, some fish hooks hanging over the fireplace and a lone harpoon propped against the wall. All these things were quite ordinary items for a man who harpooned whales for his living, but I was alarmed by the discovery of a peculiar object – a rectangle of rough material, damp and dirty – lying across the sea chest. At first I thought it must be a door mat. But there was a hole cut in the middle, and for the life of me I couldn't understand its purpose.

After pacing around for a while, I started to notice the cold. It was probably one o'clock in the morning and Coffin must have been right – the harpooner had made other arrangements for the night. Feeling cold and exhausted, I undressed, blew out the candle and curled up under the sheets.

It took some time to shake all the weariness from my bones. Just as I was about to slip off to the Land of Nod, there was a thud out in the hallway. I opened my eyes in horror. There was another thud, and another. They were footsteps. I peeped over the sheets and saw a light under the door.

"It's the head merchant," I gasped. My first reaction was to pull the covers up. When I summoned the courage to pull them down again, I saw the door swing open and a candle bobbing through the darkness. But the man placed it on the floor before I got a look at him, and started to rummage around in his sack. All I could see was the dim shape of his body and its menacing silhouette on the wall. I thought I would wait to get a glimpse of his face before making my presence known, but when he swung around and lifted the candle to his chin I almost swallowed my tongue in horror.

His face was purple and yellow, criss-crossed with thick black lines and devilish designs. At first I thought he'd been in a fight and was terribly bruised and cut – the landlord had put me in bed with a back-street brawler. Then I remembered a story I'd heard of a whale man, captured and tattooed by South Sea cannibals. This poor man must have suffered the same fate. It was only his appearance that unnerved me. And, after all, a man can be honest in

21

any kind of skin. The purple tone to his complexion must be from exposure to the fierce tropical sun, I told myself.

My bed-sharer reached into his sack and pulled out a huge tomahawk, which glinted in the candlelight. Then he reached up to the beaver skin hat he was wearing and dropped it onto the foot of the bed. Once again, I felt panic shooting from my toes to my finger tips. The harpooner's head was shaved clean, apart from a strange knot of hair dangling from the top of his scalp.

If this poor sailor had been unlucky enough to be kidnapped by cannibals, what was he doing with a tomahawk and a devilish haircut? I was so terrified I couldn't open my mouth to speak. There was a window in one corner of the room and I think I would have thrown myself through it if we hadn't been two floors up. As I quivered under the covers, the phantom began to undress, ready to hop into bed. With each piece of clothing he removed I saw more tattoos. His skin was patterned all over, and now I guessed at the truth. He was a savage, a stowaway on a boat from some cannibal island, and he was living here in the disguise of a harpooner. He was probably collecting more heads to sell, and look at that tomahawk...

Before I could shriek out, he put the weapon to his lips, lifted the candle to one end and blew out a huge cloud of smoke. The hatchet must have been hollow as it served as the savage's pipe. Then he snuffed out the candle and sprang onto the bed,

22

reaching for the sheets.

I let out a scream.

"Who the devil are you?" he roared in a strange accent, trying to grab hold of me.

"Landlord!" I screeched. "Help, anyone, come and save me!"

The tomahawk flashed in the air and I ran for the door. Coffin was standing there holding a lamp.

"Don't be afraid," he said with a smile. "Queequeg here won't harm a hair on your head."

"Stop grinning," I boomed. "You could have told me you were putting me in with a cannibal."

"He's an islander, that's all," chuckled Coffin. "Queequeg," he called over my shoulder, "if you don't mind, this man will sleep here tonight?"

"I understand," said Queequeg with a grunt. He had lit the candle and was sitting up in bed, puffing on his tomahawk pipe. "You get in," he added, motioning me to the bed.

I studied him for a moment. He had a dignified, stately look about him, and I felt a little silly for being scared of him. He was a man like me, no better and no worse.

"You can go, Landlord," I said. "It's high time I got some sleep."

23

Queequeg held the covers back for me to climb in and retreated to the other side of the bed. I blew out the candle and never slept better in my life.

My Pagan Friend

I woke with bright sunlight in my eyes and Queequeg's tattooed arm pinning me to the mattress. But there was no threat of violence from my bedfellow – he was sound asleep. He had simply rolled over in the night, and trapped me unknowingly. I twisted away from him and felt a scratch on my leg. Throwing aside the sheets I found the tomahawk lying there next to me.

"Queequeg," I cried. "Wake up and get this weapon out of our bed at once."

The harpooner opened his eyes, shook himself all over like a dog just out of the water, and sat bolt upright. He glanced at me, trying to remember why there was someone sharing his room. Then, seizing the tomahawk, he jumped to the floor. As soon as he'd hidden the strange, bladed pipe in his sack, he reached for his tall beaver hat and dropped it on his head. Then he found his boots and, after struggling with them for a few minutes, managed to jam his feet into them. The trousers and his waistcoat were the last items in his reverse dressing. I didn't think there was anything left to surprise me after watching this performance, but I was mistaken. He suddenly grabbed his harpoon, twisted the steel head from the wooden shaft and stepped over to the water bowl. Rubbing some soap onto his cheeks, he began shaving with the razor-sharp edge of the harpoon blade. Once clean-cheeked, he put on a heavy wool jacket, reassembled his harpoon and marched out into the hall carrying the tool of his trade before him.

I dressed in a hurry, curious about where the islander was going with his whale lance and wondering if there might be some trouble brewing for the landlord. But, when I entered the dining room ten minutes later, I found Queequeg at the head of a table of hungry sailors, all digging into their breakfasts. He had brought the harpoon to use as his knife. I saw him swing the barbed blade the full length of the table and hook up a bloody steak from a tin platter. He flicked the lance over the heads of the other eaters – brushing perilously close to their ears and noses I thought – and dropped the steak onto his own plate.

He was so relaxed and masterful doing this, there was something almost kingly about it.

After breakfast, I went out for a stroll. New Bedford was no prettier than it had been the night before, and after an hour or two of dismal sightseeing, the icy wind drove me back to the comforts of *The Spouter Inn*. I stepped into the lounge room to warm myself in front of the fire and saw

Queequeg sitting at a table, whittling at a small wooden figure. His brow was knitted in concentration – almost devotion – as he worked. I guessed that the little statue must be an icon or religious object, and I watched in fascination as he carved. Finally, my curiosity got the better of me and I tried to ask him what he was doing.

"Do you share my room again tonight?" he replied to my questioning.

"I would like to," I told him.

"Then we are brothers," he exclaimed, and grabbing hold of my head he pressed his forehead to mine. Next, he fetched his tomahawk pipe and we shared a friendly smoke while the rain drummed on the windows and hissed in the chimney. When the pipe had gone out, he led me up to our room and lit a small fire in the grate. I watched, wide-eyed, as he took the doormat from the sea chest and pulled it over his head. Sitting cross-legged on the floor in this strange costume, he took a ship's biscuit from his jacket pocket and held it to the flames. Queequeg motioned for me to join him in this peculiar ceremony, and set the wooden icon in front of the fire. Then he crumbled the scorched biscuit into pieces and piled them around the statue – as an offering, I supposed. Finally, he lifted the little wooden figure to his lips and kissed it, then passed it to me.

Although I was bewildered by the events of the last hour, I didn't want to offend him, and I saw no reason why my own God should object to me paying respect to another man's beliefs. So, I nodded to the wooden icon and kissed it on its nose. If I was to go whaling and learn something about the variety of this world, I couldn't be narrow-minded before I'd even left dry land. My new friend explained that we were now "united" and, if we ever faced danger together, he would gladly die to save me. We spent the rest of the day chatting and lounging in our room, while he told me something of his past.

He was born on the tropical island of Kokovok in the South Pacific, no less than 20,000 nautical miles from the freezing Atlantic port of New Bedford. As I had suspected from his straight-backed poise and kingly bearing, his father was a High Chief, and Queequeg had royal blood flowing in his veins. In his youth, he had always dreamed of seeing a wider world than his square mile of greenery surrounded by ocean and, when a whaling ship arrived one day to replace lost timber, he pleaded with the captain to let him join the crew. But the captain had a full company and he refused. Instead of sulking, Queequeg rowed out to sea and hid in a mangrove swamp which the whale ship had to pass as it departed the island. As the ship glided by, Queequeg darted out to its side in his canoe and clambered up a chain. Once he was on deck he grabbed hold of one of the steel rings bolted to the planks and swore not to let go, even if threatened with death. The captain took a cutlass and rested it on Queequeg's wrists but the islander didn't flinch. At last, the captain relented, but only on the condition that Queequeg worked as a common sailor. Despite his royal status, he accepted gladly.

"I wanted to learn from other races," he explained, "the skills and knowledge to make life easier for my own people."

Queequeg had believed that the great ships and riches of the western sailors he'd met made them more content than his own people. But, after a year or two in a whaleboat, he realized that his own tribe was as happy as any other, and he gave up the notion.

"But I still want to see more of the oceans," he told me, "before I go home to be king."

"Then you're going whaling again?" I cried. "But that's why I'm here too. I'm bound for Nantucket to find a ship."

"We'll go together," said Queequeg, smiling. "Remember, we are brothers now."

He rummaged in his sack until he found his tobacco pouch, then pulled out a handful of silver coins from it and dumped them on the floor. "Thirty dollars," he said proudly, and carefully split the pile in two, pushing one half towards me.

"I couldn't take your money, Queequeg," I protested.

For his answer, he stuffed the coins into my shirt pocket and shook my hand. "Brothers," he repeated, "until the end."

The next morning, we paid our bill and set off together for the Nantucket clipper.

The small island of Nantucket lies thirty miles off the mainland, surrounded by storms, squalls and sailboats. It is the heart of the American whaling industry and the hardy Quakers who've settled there have pledged their lives to service on the oceans. Indeed, these fishermen spend more time at sea than they do at home on their island. A whaling voyage usually lasts for three years, sometimes four, and a sailor will be lucky if he touches land in all that time.

Whalers carry everything they need in the holds of their ships, including all their food and drinking water, sealed up in casks.

The voyage on the clipper was rough but bracing and, when we landed in the early evening, both of us had hearty appetites. Peter Coffin had recommended *The Try Pots Inn* and, when at last we found its sign among the whitewashed wooden houses of the port, supper was already being served. After three huge bowls of steaming-hot clam chowder, a thick soup that tasted as fresh as the sea, we went straight to our beds and slept soundly.

In the morning, Queequeg had an announcement to make.

"Yojo has told me that you must choose the ship we sail on."

I stared at him in amazement. "Yojo" was the name of his wooden idol.

"But I don't know anything about whale ships," I cried.

"You will make the right choice."

Twenty minutes of argument did me no good. Yojo had made his decision and I had to go along with it. Reluctantly, I struck out alone that morning, my mission to find us a suitable berth.

But one thing I knew already was that old sailors love to chat. I soon discovered from a wrinkled seadog sitting in a rocking chair that there was a ship called the *Pequod* recruiting for a three-year voyage. When I got down to the dock, I was amazed at the sight of her. She was at least fifty years old, and her wooden body was worn smooth from a thousand gales and sun-scorched voyages. The original masts had been torn away in a typhoon off Japan and replaced with an eastern wood, white as salt. All along the bulwarks – the waist-high sides of the ship – the six-inch-long teeth of sperm whales had been fixed as rope ties, so that it looked as though the decks were ringed with gaping whale jaws. Everywhere I looked there were bleached ivory bones from the *Pequod's* prey. The tiller itself was constructed from a single piece of a whale's jaw. As I gazed at the strange ship I heard a step behind me.

"What's your business here?"

I turned to see an elderly sailor, tanned and grizzled, stalking the deck. He wore a captain's uniform.

"I'm here to sign up to go whaling," I told him confidently. "And see the world while I'm at it."

There was a sudden glint in his eye. "And what do you know about whaling?"

"Nothing, sir."

"I thought so," he declared with satisfaction.

"But I'm ready to learn."

"Have you had a look at Captain Ahab?" he asked craftily.

"Who's he?"

"The captain of this ship, of course."

"But I thought you were the captain."

"No," he snarled. "I am Captain Peleg, part owner of the *Pequod* and responsible for getting her shipshape for the next voyage. Ahab is her captain. And, since his last voyage, Ahab has only one leg. That should teach you about whaling."

"Was the other one lost to a whale?" I asked in a whisper.

"Lost?" he roared. "No man, not lost. It was devoured, chewed up, crunched to splinters by the most terrible whale ever to spout water. Have you even been to sea before?"

"I've worked four voyages in merchant ships, sir."

He grimaced as though in disgust. "Don't mention the merchant service to me, boy. Merchant ships ply from port to port and are rarely out of sight of land. In a whale ship you're gone for three years, and you might sail around the globe ten times without stepping ashore."

"I know, sir. Didn't I say I wanted to see the world?"

He waved me forward with a gnarled and weather-lined hand. "Step over to the starboard side and tell me what you see," he ordered.

I wasn't sure if he was playing a joke on me but I obeyed. The ship was pointing to the open sea, and I studied the flat horizon and the endless swell of waves rolling off across the deep.

"Nothing out there but water," I reported when he called me back.

"Aye, and now you've seen the world," he said with a snort of laughter.

"I still want to go whaling, sir," I cried, irritated by his tricks.

Perhaps Peleg was surprised or impressed with my determination because now his eyes softened and a new note of respect entered his voice.

"Are you sure, lad?"

"I am. And I know a fine harpooner who will ship with me."

"Excellent," he cried, clasping his hands together. "If you come tomorrow, I will sign you up and we can discuss your lay."

Queequeg had explained to me that a whaling crew was paid in shares of the final profit from the voyage – a lay. I thanked the captain and rushed down the gangplank to tell my friend the good news. But as soon as I reached the dock I remembered that it is a sailor's custom to have a look at his captain before he commits himself to a voyage. It's wise to have some idea of the man you are about to serve under for so many months or years, out in the loneliness of the ocean.

"Captain Peleg, sir," I called, climbing the gangplank. "Perhaps I should go and pay my respects to Captain Ahab."

"Oh, don't bother yourself with that," he answered, slapping my shoulder with one of his great hands. "In truth, Ahab hasn't been too well and he's confined to his house. But he'll be fit by the day you sail, never fear."

"What kind of a man is he, sir?"

"A great man," said Peleg, "an extraordinary man. Ahab's been in colleges, and among the cannibals, and seen more wonders than most men could begin

34

to imagine. He's the finest harpooner in all the islands and a first-rate captain. It's true that since he lost his leg he's been a little moody and fierce, but that will pass once he gets out to sea again and back to his work. And if he does strike you as gruff, try to think of the terrors he went through when he lost his limb. Ask yourself if you would not be gruff yourself, in his position."

With these words ringing in my ears, I ran back to the inn.

To Sea

Queequeg and I spent the next two days lounging in our rooms, eating and sleeping in preparation for the voyage ahead of us. Once we were aboard, there would be no more soft pillows or fine lunches for three long years and we wanted to stock up on our comforts. While we relaxed, the *Pequod* was swarming with tradesmen and workers, filling her hold with the cargo she needed for her voyage. Fresh sails were fixed to the masts and new coils of rope stored for the rigging. Lumber and tools were stashed away, along with every conceivable spare part for the whaleboats themselves – the slender craft that are sent out to chase the whale. Each ship carried three or four of them, lashed to her decks or tied in the rigging. On top of all this they piled cloth, nails, oil and straw. Then came the casks of provisions: dried beef, biscuit, bread, water and rum. I have to confess, I was more than a little nervous at the prospect of spending three years at sea, never stopping at a friendly port. What would it be like walking on solid ground after a thousand days of swaying on the waves? But this was the reason for the heavy cargo the *Pequod* carried; she had to be completely self-sufficient, a speck of self-sustaining industry on the stark ocean plains.

Now and again, I would saunter down to the docks to see if Captain Ahab had joined the ship. Each time I inquired after him I was told he would be along shortly. On the fourth day, all sailors were ordered to be on deck just after dawn and so I knew we must be sailing at last.

It was misty and cold as we hurried down to the docks the next morning, carrying our sea sacks across our shoulders. As we turned around a stack of crates, I noticed five or six men running ahead, wrapped in the fog. The light was too dim to see their faces. They were wearing odd-looking clothes and strange hats. Approaching the *Pequod* they vanished into the shadows and I wondered if I might still have been dreaming.

By the time we'd stored our kit in the forecastle, where the sailors sleep, the sun was up and the decks of the ship were bustling with men. In the afternoon, Captain Peleg came aboard and ordered us to cast all lines away. Then he guided us out into the open water.

"But where is our captain?" I asked a Chinese sailor rushing by.

"He keeps to his cabin," the man answered. "Perhaps the air is too cold for him up here."

It was true that the day was drawing on and all the heat had gone from the air. I watched as the ship's prow plunged into the great ocean waves, the water drops so cold they felt like ice pellets when they stung my face. With three cheers from the sailors, Captain Peleg climbed down to a launch that would take him back to shore, and we struck off alone, due south into the Atlantic wilderness. It was Christmas Day, and my voyage on the whale ship *Pequod* had finally begun.

For a week we were blown about and frost-bitten by the fierce North Atlantic weather, but we were gradually creeping closer to the warmth of the tropics. At first I ran about doing my work wrapped in my jacket and with a thick pair of moccasins on my feet. But, as the ocean slowly turned a deep sapphire and the sun lingered in the sky a little longer each day, I was soon in short sleeves and going without shoes. It was good to be back at sea again, and the *Pequod* was a fine ship with a strong crew.

The first mate was a well-built 30-year-old Nantucketer named Starbuck. He was a brilliant harpooner and known for his bravery, but he was cautious too.

"I will have no man in my boat," he announced to us all, "who is not afraid of a whale."

Starbuck was a practical whaler. He didn't like to risk his life – or that of his crew – any more than was necessary, and had already lost his father and brother to the violence of his profession. Above all he was a loyal man – loyal to his Quaker faith, to his men and to his captain.

The second mate was Stubb, an uncomplicated, happy-go-lucky sailor from Cape Cod. He'd battled with so many whales he was calm, even relaxed, in the chase. He'd be puffing away at his pipe with one hand, and ready to launch his harpoon with the other, while most sailors were shaking with fear.

Flask was the third mate and he hailed from Martha's Vineyard, another whaling island south of Nantucket. He was a short and simple man, but as brave as the others.

Each mate captained his own whaleboat, manned by four men working the oars and a harpooner standing in the prow. The harpooners held a special status in the hierarchy of the ship. They were the elite whalers, skilled and fearless hunters. To recognize this, they were given a much greater lay than the common sailors.

Aside from my friend Queequeg, the other harpooners were Tashtego and Daggoo. Tashtego was a Gay-Head American Indian with jet-black hair falling to his shoulders and high, noble cheekbones. His ancestors had hunted game in the wild American forests with their bows and arrows. Now Tashtego hunted in the oceans with his lance. Daggoo was an African, strong as a lion, standing six foot five in his socks.

The rest of the crew was made up of sailors from all corners of the Earth. Whaling was an international business and the *Pequod* carried a selection of the people of the world, all dedicated to the pursuit of oil.

For the first week at sea there was no sign of our captain. The mates took care of the running of the ship, navigating her towards the established whaling grounds to the south. It was quite usual for a captain to remain in his cabin until the ship had reached a cruising position, but I was so curious about the mysterious Ahab and his lost limb, I was desperate to get a look at him. Each time I came up from the forecastle, I glanced behind me to see if the captain was up on the quarterdeck – the raised deck at the stern of the ship reserved for officers and the man at the tiller. Each time I was disappointed, until one morning I clambered up the ladder into the air and a shiver of apprehension ran down my back. Captain Ahab stood directly behind me.

My first impression was that he was a man cast in

iron. He was tall and perhaps sixty years old. His skin was brown and leathery from decades of roasting in the tropics, but it was his straight-backed and determined posture that made me think of an iron man. I had never seen a more wilful, resolute expression set on a human face. I would sooner have had an argument with a snow-topped mountain peak than with this proud-looking master of the oceans. He glowered at me and then stared out to sea, as though he owned the waves and was surveying his property.

As he turned his head, I noticed a silver scar or mark on his skin. It emerged from the grizzled hair on his head and snaked across his sun-scorched face, to disappear under his collar. The men argued over this oddity, some saying Ahab had been struck by lightning like an old oak tree and branded for life, others that it was a sinister birth mark, and stretched from his crown to his sole.

So striking was his appearance, at first I didn't notice the white leg upon which he leaned; it was a piece of whale ivory, hacked from a leviathan's jaw bone. Ahab had ordered the ship's carpenter to bore him a special hole in the quarterdeck, about the depth of a thimble. The tip of his ivory leg rested neatly in this mooring hole, giving the captain more stability in rough weather. The whale bone was an ugly and constant reminder of the agent of his injury and it must have been painful to wear. Each time he moved, he seemed to grimace and snarl. But, at the same moment, I also saw in those flinty eyes some trace of sadness, like a man in mourning, who has lost the thing he loves most and refuses to be comforted.

So this was my captain, many things in one man.

As we neared the tropics, Ahab spent more time at his lookout on the quarterdeck, until he was posted there from dawn to dusk. His expression was always the same: alert and determined, but heartbroken somehow. I could sense him prowling everywhere about the ship, haunting us like a restless ghost. In the depths of the night I heard the knock of his ivory foot pacing about on the planks. Some of the men began to whisper that he never closed his eyes to sleep. The steward told me that the captain wandered the ship at all hours, visiting secret chambers and compartments where he could be heard talking to himself. Whether this was true or not, it was clear to me that Ahab was a troubled man. One morning he sent me to fetch his stool and pipe from his cabin, so that he could smoke on deck while studying the horizon. When he was seated and puffing away, I turned to go back to my work when I heard him grunt in surprise.

"What's this?" he muttered, staring at the pipe. "Your smoke no longer soothes me."

I was about to ask him if I could bring him something else from his cabin, when he hurled the pipe into the waves. It hissed and bubbled before sinking out of sight.

"Pipes are for the happy, contented man," he growled, "for the comfy chair by the fire, for the day's work over and a night's rest to come. That serenity is not for the likes of me. I'll smoke no more, sailor."

And with that he waved me away.

Every man aboard the *Pequod* noticed that their captain seemed brooding and ill at ease. It made them anxious for the success of the voyage. As the days passed, it began to feel as if we were sharing the decks with a rumbling volcano. Every sailor feared his wrath. We knew that whatever fire was in him, it would soon have to explode to the surface. But when it did, none of us could have guessed how terrible it would be.

Ahab's Rage

One afternoon, after long hours spent rubbing his face and gazing out to sea, Ahab called Starbuck to his side.

"All hands on deck," he said softly.

The mate blinked in surprise. This was an order so rarely given that he thought he'd misheard his captain. Ahab repeated the command.

"Sailors assemble on the mid-deck," shouted Starbuck and, from every corner of the ship, the bemused men came running, wondering if they were sinking or in the grip of some other calamity. When we'd gathered in a semicircle, our captain paced up and down in front of us for a full minute before speaking.

"What do you do when you see a whale, men?" he hissed suddenly.

"We sing out," the sailors yelled.

"That's good," said Ahab with a roar. I felt a rush of excitement when I heard his voice and the other men felt it too, because we all crowded forward to hear what he would say next.

"And what then?" he shouted, his eyes flashing.

"Lower away and row after him," we answered.

"And what do you sing while you row?"

"A dead whale or a sunk boat," came the shout.

With each cry our captain seemed to shudder with some passion, and his energy was infectious. Every sailor was staring intently at him now.

"Do you see this, lads?" he called, holding up a bright, gold coin glistening in the sun. "It's a Spanish doubloon, sixteen dollars worth of solid gold. Do you see it? Fetch me a hammer, Mister Starbuck."

While the first mate dashed off for the tool, Ahab rubbed the coin on his waistcoat until it gleamed even brighter. The gold disc burned like a ring of fire, snatched from the sun. When Starbuck came back with the hammer, Ahab took it, stepped into our ranks, and moved to the main mast.

"Whosoever among you sights a white whale," he cried, "a sperm whale with a wrinkled brow and a crooked jaw, he shall have this ounce of Spanish gold."

He took a nail from his waistcoat pocket and hammered the coin to the mast at head height.

"Look sharp for him," said Ahab, spinning around to face us, "and crack your lungs with shouting when you sight him."

"Captain Ahab," cried Tashtego, "is this the White Whale, the creature some men call Moby Dick?"

"The same," hissed Ahab.

"With bent and rusting harpoons sticking out of him?" asked Queequeg.

"And a strange spout of misty water?" added Daggoo.

"The very whale we want," answered Ahab, clenching his fists. "And Moby Dick is his name."

"But captain," cried Starbuck, pushing through the throng of sailors, "was it this Moby Dick that took off your leg?"

Ahab gritted his teeth and glowered at the first mate. Then, controlling himself, he raised his arms and motioned the crew closer. "Men, it's true that he was the one who dismasted me. Moby Dick brought me to this dead stump I stand upon before you. I will chase him," he said, spitting out the words, "around both Capes, and through storms, whirlpools and flames if needs be. I will never stop chasing him. And this is what you've signed up for, lads." His voice was a shout now. "To stab that white whale until he rolls dead in the water and spouts no more. So, will you help me?"

The crew whooped and shouted in their excitement. "Aye, aye," they called. "Death to Moby Dick!"

"God bless you," Ahab cried. "Steward, fetch some

grog for these men. But Mister Starbuck, what's that long face for? Won't you join in our hunt?"

"I will join any hunt," the mate began in a firm voice, stepping closer to his captain, "that is my proper business. But I am here to chase whales, not work my commander's vengeance on a dumb animal."

"I have good reason to hate that animal," answered Ahab, "and I will have my revenge. No man can prevent it."

"It makes no sense to hate a simple, unreasoning beast," Starbuck continued. "It's like being angry with the wind for blowing you over, or with the rain for making you wet."

"But angry I am," roared Ahab, "and, while I have the power to destroy the creature that maimed me, you may count on it that I will." Ahab rested a hand on his mate's shoulder and drew him close. "The crew are with me, Starbuck. See how they thrill to the chase. What is it to you anyway, killing one animal, when you've already harpooned hundreds? Would you mutiny against your captain, when all I ask is that you kill one more?"

"But how will you find him, sir?" Starbuck protested. "It might take years to find one individual whale in all the world's oceans. It is an impossible search."

"I have charts," replied the captain, "of every bit of water he could hide in. I have maps of this watery world he calls home. By plotting every reported sighting of him over the last twenty years, I have discovered his habits and his regular cruising grounds. There is still a huge area to search. It might take us months or years to find him, Starbuck – but find him we will."

"What of our duty to the owners, sir?" Starbuck appealed. "We are here to get them whale oil."

"So we shall," answered Ahab. "There is no reason why we shouldn't do our duty to them, while we pursue Moby Dick. Men," he called to the crew, "I have a mighty appetite for dead whales and we'll lower our boats whenever you sight one. It will line your wallets when you get home, and keep you in practice for our most important mission, to kill Moby Dick."

At this, the crew cheered and the first mate looked defeated. Ahab had won the argument and Starbuck turned away with downcast eyes. The steward rushed past the first mate, carrying a huge jug of rum. He halted next to Ahab, slopping the drink over the boards.

"You harpooners," bellowed Ahab, glancing over his shoulder at his silent mates and then turning to the three lancers with a look of triumph. "Come closer with your weapons."

They stepped forward and the rest of the crew closed around them in a huddle.

"Drink and pass!" ordered Ahab, handing the jug to Daggoo. Each one of us on the deck glugged on the burning rum, until the tankard was handed back to the captain.

"Now take the heads off those harpoons," he

ordered. The three lancers snapped the iron blades from their long wooden poles and held them up to the captain.

"Turn them over like wine goblets, and step forward."

The blade heads were hollow and, when the bewildered harpooners inverted them, Ahab lifted the jug and filled them to the brim with fiery rum.

"Now, drink and swear," roared Ahab. "Death to Moby Dick, or death to us all if we fail!"

With shouts and shrieks of encouragement from the crew, the harpooners whispered the vow and tilted the blade heads to their lips. Then Ahab passed the jug again and all the crew took another measure. From the corner of my drunken eye, I saw Starbuck's face go pale and a shiver take hold of him. But I was too busy laughing and shouting with the others to pay much attention to it, or to notice the victorious glance the captain gave our first mate as he retired to his private cabin.

All night long the crew of the *Pequod* drank and danced under the tropical moon. I confess I was as thrilled as the others to be sharing our captain's feud with the White Whale. While we sipped rum, some of the older sailors told stories about Moby Dick, how he had menaced the whaling fleets for years, smashing whaleboats and dragging men down into a cold ocean grave. He was a cunning and deadly enemy, so they said, tricking his hunters with sudden turns and dives just as they thought he was trapped.

They even whispered that the whale enjoyed attacking men, and must be an intelligent and evil creature to do so.

A white-haired mariner from the Isle of Man, who was more cautious — and sober — than the rest of us, told the story of a captain who went after Moby Dick in three whaleboats, off the coast of Japan. After being led far from his ship, he saw the animal dive and disappear. For ten minutes the boats bobbed close together, the crews waiting for the whale to resurface so they could continue the chase. But while they relaxed, chatting, wiping their brows and shielding their eyes from the glaring sun, Moby Dick was thundering towards them, charging up from a thousand feet below.

The speeding whale smashed into the hull of one boat and carried it forty feet into the air. It burst into a cloud of wood chips and broken, bloody men. With his whole, giant mass out of the water, the whale twisted in the air and landed his bulk on the two remaining boats. Oars and planks splintered, and the crews were crushed or drowned.

The captain, though half-drowned himself, threw his harpoon, then jumped onto the back of the attacking whale and stabbed at it with his pocket knife. That man was Ahab, enraged and defiant to the end. As he gouged so uselessly at the whale, it turned its head slowly, purposefully, and flicking its bent jaw under him, scythed away his leg.

"I met one of the sailors from that voyage in a New York drinking den," explained the Manxman.

"He told me the whole story. They fished Ahab out of the water, screaming in pain like a madman. He thrashed about so much in his rage that, for a whole month, he had to be lashed to his bed. When he was calm again at last, the crew thought everything was back to normal. But, after what I've seen today, I believe Ahab was only hiding his frenzied hate for the whale, locking it away in his heart to stop anyone from getting suspicious of his plans. Shipmates, I reckon he's been plotting for months to come back and kill Moby Dick, waiting patiently to be given command of a ship. It's a madness, I tell you. He'll stop at nothing to catch this whale. And we're at risk of being consumed by the same madness and hate that has possessed our captain."

But we were too busy drinking and dancing to heed the old sailor's warning. With our heads full of rum, we didn't fear any living creature. We thought we were invincible.

Five Phantoms

It was a full three days before my head stopped aching from the excesses of that rum-sodden night. But our voyage went on as before. The ship pushed south under heavy, storm-threatening skies, with a sailor at the top of each mast keeping a lookout for whales – and for one whale in particular.

All of the crew had to take their turns as lookouts at the mast head, and I admit I had been dreading the experience ever since we left Nantucket. In a whaling ship, lookouts are so vital to the success of the voyage, they are sent up the rigging in storms or sunshine, from the moment the ship leaves port until a few minutes before she ties up at the close of her voyage. On the *Pequod*, there were no luxuries like a crow's nest, where a sailor can sit snug and safe. Our lookouts balanced their feet on two thin wooden spars that jutted out from each mast, holding onto the rigging with aching fingers while the ship swayed below. The first time I tried an hour at the mast head, I felt about as comfortable as a man perched on a bucking bull's horns. But it's amazing what you can get used to. After a week or two, I was standing with my arms crossed and my back to the pendulum mast, lounging one hundred feet above the deck as if casually waiting for a friend on a sunny street corner.

Once we arrived in the tropics, I truly enjoyed my time up on the masts. It was soothing to gaze over the limitless expanse of the ocean and see it melt into the blue sky at the horizon. There were times that I had to pinch myself to stay awake, I was so relaxed by the gentle roll of the ship and the soft, tropical breezes caressing my cheeks. Needless to say, I didn't spot any whales. I was too busy dozing, studying the sky and pondering the mysteries of the universe to be of much use to the whaling industry. But I knew what to do in case I did see a leviathan, cruising on the lid of the sea. "There she blows!" was the customary cry. I will never forget the first time I heard those words, and the thrill that surged through me before the shout had faded.

"There she blows," howled Tashtego, leaning away from the mast and with his left arm stretched out as a pointer. "A whole school of them. About two miles off our starboard bow."

Instantly, the ship was buzzing with commotion. Tashtego climbed down to the decks and joined the other harpooners as we winched the three whaleboats over the side and prepared to launch them.

I was in Starbuck's crew, fumbling with the lowering ropes, when I heard a gasp from another sailor. Spinning around, I saw five phantoms helping Ahab down the stairs from the quarterdeck. Their clothes were made of black silk and their skin was as yellow as tiger fur.

The sight of these strangers was even more shocking to me than the cry from the lookout. When the group was on the main deck, four of the men ran across to the spare whaleboat and swung her out over the water. Ahab waited with the fifth man, the master of the others. He wore a high turban made of his own, pleated white hair, and a single, bent tooth poked out from between his pale lips.

"Lower away there," Ahab called to the sailors. "All of you into your boats."

We leaped down the ship's side and into the pitching whaleboats.

"Pull away," boomed Flask, working the steering oar in the back of his boat.

"Pull, my little ones," coaxed Stubb.

"On lads, let's pull 'till you break your backs," called Starbuck over my head.

But, as the three boats moved away from the *Pequod*, the fourth darted out from behind the stern of the ship and overtook us. The phantoms were rowing like wild men, with our own captain standing at the rear.

"Is it Ahab?" muttered Starbuck in his amazement.

"The old man's still hungry for the chase," laughed Stubb.

"Aye," cried Flask. "And he's brought his own crew along. They must have been hidden in the ship all this time."

With a shudder, I remembered the dark shadows that had flitted before Queequeg and myself as we walked down to board the ship in Nantucket. Then there were the whispers of Ahab talking to himself, in secret chambers below decks. I saw Starbuck shaking his head as he stood over us.

"Five more hands, that's all, Mister Starbuck," called Stubb calmly, looking across at the first mate. "If they're here to help, I've no complaints. Now men," he said to his own crew, "don't row too hard. Just hard enough to split your lungs, but no harder. Pull until your eyes pop out. What's this? Has someone dropped an anchor over the side? Are we stuck? Pull when you're ready, lads. Pull until you burst a blood vessel."

"Let's not get left behind," cried Starbuck, rousing himself. "There are whales to catch today, and that's why we're here."

With the mates coaxing and threatening their crews in a strange chatter of oaths and entreaties, we rowed until our hearts pounded and the sweat ran down our faces. But we couldn't catch Ahab and his boat of tigers. They worked as though they were whipped on, their arms pumping like steel pistons.

We were making for the spot where Tashtego had last sighted the whales, when there was a sudden shout from Ahab.

"They've sounded. Ship your oars."

Queequeg had explained to me that "sounding" was when the whale dives below the waves, disappearing for a few seconds or as long as an hour. The animal only comes to the surface to breathe or mate, spending most of his time underwater. We lifted our oars out of the water and rested. Somewhere beneath us, in all those billions of gallons of brine, the whales were swimming. I thought of the old mariner's story and shuddered to think that a furious leviathan might be aiming straight for us as we bobbed like apples on the surface. But Queequeg finally broke the silence with a cry.

"They're up again, over here, sir."

I saw a wash of bubbles and mist burst onto the surface of the water, then Starbuck turned our boat.

"Pull on, men, we're the nearest. Let's get our prize."

The sea was swelling now, with great waves lifting us up on their crests and then flinging us down into a hollow. After ten minutes in the chase, there was no sign of the other whaleboats or the *Pequod,* and I saw a blanket of dark clouds spreading above us. But we rowed on with all our hearts.

"Pull, lads. We're almost close enough for a strike," encouraged Starbuck.

"There's a squall coming up fast, sir," yelled one of the crew.

"Time to kill a whale before any squall catches us," answered the mate. "Up you get, harpooner."

Queequeg jumped to his feet and was at the prow of the boat in a flash. I looked out at the sea, but there was so much spray and mist I could only see a few feet in any direction. But I could hear the whale just ahead of us, making an ear-splitting slosh of water as it parted the waves.

"Throw, man," boomed Starbuck.

Queequeg's broad, tattooed back tensed and his arm snapped the harpoon into the air. At once there was a fierce shove from the back of the boat and, at the front, it was as though we'd run aground on an underwater cliff. I heard one of the oars cracking and the sail coming down, then there was a gush of steam shooting up next to me and a deafening rumble below the planks.

The harpoon had only grazed the whale and, in his surprise, he had slapped us with his mighty tail. He had dived and escaped, and we were left in the grip of the squall. It was roaring, forking and crackling around us like a lightning storm on the prairie. For an hour we were tossed around in high waves and a gale of a wind. When the squall at last moved off, we were left half-drowned, the boat was leaking and we had drifted miles away from our comrades.

It was a miserable night. Starbuck lit the waterproof lantern and tied it to the tip of the splintered mast. Then we waited, alone on a choppy sea. We were up to our knees in water, and had to keep bailing to prevent the boat from sinking. By dawn, a cold mist had curled around us. We were too tired to speak. Suddenly, Queequeg lifted a cupped hand to his ear. I noticed a faint sound of creaking and the distant clank of a chain.

"Over the side with you," yelled Starbuck, pushing me into the sea.

I thought the mate had gone mad, but then I saw the huge prow of the *Pequod* poking out of the fog, less than twenty feet away. It rolled over the abandoned whaleboat as I swam clear with the other sailors.

Our boat surfaced at the stern of the ship and we grabbed hold of it, calling to our friends. They threw lines down to us and helped us up the side chains.

It was my first day of real whaling. Starbuck was supposed to be the safest mate on the ship, yet even he had continued the chase for a whale in the face of a violent squall. I had survived a night in the open, a capsizing and a ramming by my own ship. I studied the other men from my boat, sipping hot tea and chatting with Stubb about the weather. This was nothing out of the ordinary for them.

"Come, Queequeg," I called. "I want you to step

down to the forecastle with me. I am in the business of whaling now, so I must draw up my last will and testimony, and you are to witness it."

When this was done, I joined the others for some tea, feeling much better about things. I was a proper whale man now and ready for anything.

Strange Sightings

The *Pequod* sailed on in fair weather. We had already slipped past the whaling grounds of the Azores and the Cape Verde Islands, and soon we passed through the warm waters off the coast of Brazil. But there were no more sightings, and so Ahab turned his ship to the east, to the Cape of Good Hope.

A few days after they'd first shown themselves, the men who formed Ahab's crew came out on deck to eat their meals and get some fresh air. They didn't talk much with us common sailors, but from a few snatched words with them, we learned that they hailed from the islands around Manila and had been hired in Nantucket with the sole purpose of hunting the White Whale. Their master with the turban made from his own hair was called Fedallah, and they hinted that he had mysterious powers, including the gift of prophecy. He moved silently around the ship, staring out to sea and never speaking with anyone except his own men or Ahab. Although he was only slight, there was a concentrated menace about him that reminded me of a king cobra about to strike. I kept my distance from Fedallah.

It was all very exotic and peculiar to me, but the other whalers were more worldly and experienced; they accepted our new passengers without any questions or fuss.

When we neared the tip of Africa, the Cape winds began howling all around us. The waves grew higher, until the *Pequod* slammed down into their furrows, sending foam racing across her decks. For a week we struggled to pass into the Indian Ocean. Cape of Good Hope they call it! Cape Torment would be a better name. Any sailor worth his salt knows that storms rage for months around these seas, blackening the skies and dismasting ships.

Once around the Cape, we cruised into the calm waters of the Indian Ocean. I was up in the masts on lookout duty when a distant sail loomed on the horizon. It was another whale ship, the *Albatross,* and she was bound home for Nantucket after almost four years at sea.

The sight of that tired old whaler filled me with wonder – was this how we would look after our own voyage was over? She had been bleached almost white by the pounding seas and burning sun. All her woodwork was scored and chipped from the ravages of heavy weather, and her rigging was furry with wear. The lookouts at the masts had beards hanging down to their chests, and their clothes were so tattered and worn they were little better than rags.

"*Albatross,*" beckoned Ahab from the quarterdeck, "have you seen the White Whale?"

The opposite captain, leaning out over his faded bulwarks, lifted a hailing trumpet to his mouth. But, as his ship lurched suddenly on a huge wave, he dropped this trumpet into the water. He cupped his hands and shouted some half-heard words above the wind. The *Albatross* hadn't sighted Moby Dick.

"Should we lower a boat for a gam, sir?" asked Starbuck, standing by Ahab's side.

A "gam" was a captain's meeting at sea, and most lonely whale ship captains were only too happy to spend an hour or two catching up on news. Even though we were at the edge of the Indian Ocean, thousands of miles from home, there might be men serving on the *Albatross* who were good friends – perhaps even relatives – of the sailors on the *Pequod*. But Ahab was no regular ship's captain.

"I wouldn't waste five minutes with a man who knows nothing of the White Whale," he whispered to his mate. Sighing, Starbuck retreated to the main deck.

Ignoring the mate's departure, Ahab leaned out into the wind. "Send all future letters for the *Pequod* to the Pacific," he called to the *Albatross*. Her captain nodded and turned away, perhaps happy that he could keep sailing for home without any interruption.

"What's all this about letters?" I asked the man next to me in amazement.

"Whale mail, friend," answered the sailor, a cockney from the cobbled streets of London. "All ships fresh out of port carry a sack of letters. When we meet another whaler at sea they check the ship names for a match. I myself had a card delivered once, after two long years at sea. And when I got it, it was so damp and green with mildew and age that it fell apart in my fingers. But, if you live long enough, you can be sure you'll get your post in the end."

He finished this sentence with a long laugh and was still chuckling twenty minutes later, when the *Albatross* and her ragged crew had vanished over the horizon.

Our ship nosed on, heading east, until we entered smooth waters covered in a vast, undulating carpet of plankton. This tiny yellow creature is the food of the right whale, and it spread across the ocean for miles around the bows of the *Pequod*, like a golden field of wheat. The next day we saw dozens of right whales, cruising through the plankton with their mouths agape, filtering the creatures through their strange gills. This whale has hundreds of long, stiff bristles which trap the plankton when it closes its mouth. These bristles were used to stiffen ladies' corsets, and it was unsettling to think of fashionable women lacing themselves up inside what used to be a whale's mouth.

Right whales were hunted by some whalers, but they were considered small fry by Nantucket ships. The *Pequod* and her kind preferred to hunt the sperm whale. One of the mightiest of all whales, each animal could provide up to one hundred barrels of high quality oil. We sailed on.

One morning, as the *Pequod* glided through the fields of plankton in the direction of the isle of Java, Daggoo let out a fearsome scream from his post on the mast head.

"There she blows! It's Moby Dick, dead ahead."

As usual, Ahab was pacing the quarterdeck a hundred feet below. He sighted the great, snow-white mass of blubber lying on the sea and burst into action. "Lower away," he commanded, and the four boats shot off across the waves, with his own crew of tigers taking the lead.

But, when we reached the place of the sighting, the animal had disappeared. We waited in our boats until there was a murmur below us, and then a vast, pulpy shape, unlike anything I'd ever seen, bobbed up and floated lifelessly on the surface. It was at least one hundred feet wide and seemed to be made of a thousand long arms like jungle creepers, twisting and

writhing in the sea. With the same strange murmur we had heard before, it slowly sank out of sight.

"I'd rather fight the White Whale than see such a foul thing," whispered Starbuck. "It's bad luck for us all."

"What was it, sir?" I asked him.

"The dead carcass of a giant squid," he replied firmly. "They say only a few men ever see one and reach home to tell of it. The sperm whale dives to the bottom to hunt and eat them. I've seen the scars from their hooked tentacles imprinted on a whale's blubbery skin, but I've never seen one in the flesh before. And I wish I hadn't. Such monsters belong to the private world of the whale."

His words made my blood run cold. We followed Ahab's boat back to the ship in silence.

The Shark Massacre

Starbuck might have trembled at the sight of the giant squid, but to Queequeg it was a good omen.

"When you see a squid," he told me, honing the blade of his harpoon on a whetstone, "you'll soon see a sperm whale." He was not mistaken.

The next day was hot and calm, and the crew lolled about the decks. I was sent up the mast on lookout duty but, after an hour of the gentle swaying of the ship and breathing the perfumed air of the tropics, I could hardly keep my eyes open. I came to with a start, my mind saving me just as my knees were sagging and my body was about to crash down onto the deck. I rubbed my eyes. Off the port bow, an enormous sperm whale was rolling in the water like the capsized hull of a battleship. As I opened my mouth to cry out, he spouted a huge jet of water. Every man on the ship was staring at him.

"Clear away the boats," came the call from Ahab, and a minute later we were out on the ocean, rowing with all our strength.

As we approached the whale, he caught sight of us and dived. But, a moment later, he surfaced close to

Stubb's boat and started crashing through the waves.

"After him, men," cried Stubb. "Row like thunder."

I saw Tashtego leap into the front of Stubb's boat and hurl his harpoon. It caught fast in the side of the whale, and we all heard a sudden crack. It was the "line" – the thick rope that is fixed to the harpoon – taking up the strain. Each boat carried over a thousand feet of the line, carefully coiled in a wooden drum called the line tub. If the whale dives deep, another line can be fixed to the first, but the sailor who does the knotting has to be careful. When the whale swims away the line goes hissing through the air, fast enough to slice a man in two.

Stubb's boat was towed along behind the injured animal, with all his crew holding onto the oar locks for dear life. Tashtego ducked down and let the mate push past him to the prow. As soon as the whale began to tire, Stubb stabbed at it with a long lance. "Haul in," he cried, and his crew tugged on the line until the boat was so close to the whale that the mate could have stepped onto its back. He probed with the bloody lance until he found its heart, and at last the whale rolled in a red tide of its own blood and died.

"He's gone, Mister Stubb," said Tashtego.

"Aye," answered the mate, "he'll swim no more." He stood at the prow of the boat, lost in thought, gazing at the huge creature he had just destroyed.

The other boats came up and each sank a line into the dead whale. Even with sixteen men pulling on the oars, it took us several hours to drag the massive corpse to the side of the ship. It was dark by the time I was standing on deck. Ahab ordered us to secure the whale for the night and then retreated to his cabin, as if in a temper.

"You'd think he'd be happy," moaned Flask. "Stubb's whale will bring him ninety barrels at least."

"He doesn't care about the oil," whispered Starbuck. "The sight of that dead whale only reminds him of the one he's really searching for."

"I don't care what he wants," roared Stubb, with a grin on his face. "It's my whale and I claim a piece of it. Daggoo, hop down there and cut me off a steak."

The whale had been chained to the side of the *Pequod*, and the harpooner had no trouble jumping down and fetching Stubb his dinner.

"I want it rare," Stubb shouted to the cook. "Lift the steak in one hand and hold a match to it with the other, then lay it on my plate."

We stood around watching the mate dig into his supper. Licking his lips and chomping at the whale meat he made quite a noise, but there was such a sloshing and splashing from the sea I could hardly hear him.

"Someone else has come for dinner," called Queequeg, standing at the bulwarks. I walked over to him and leaned out into the dark. Around the great bulk of the whale I could see the water foaming with sharks. There were hundreds of them, snapping their jaws and gorging on the corpse. In their frenzy to get to the meat, they were even biting each other, their triangular teeth flashing in the bright moonlight.

"There are so many of them," I muttered.

"We're close to the equator," replied Flask, standing next to me. "The seas are full of them here. We'd better drive them off, or by morning half our whale will be gone."

He ordered the harpooners to lean over the bulwarks and stab the sharks with whaling spades – long poles with sharp blades at their points. For an hour they butchered the sleek, black-eyed predators, until the sharks were so demented in their feeding frenzy that they tore great chunks out of each other, some even snapping at their own tails. The whole sea churned with blood. At last, the sight was so awful I couldn't watch any more and so I went down to my hammock. Even below decks, it was impossible to escape the carnage. The bodies of the sharks pounded the side of the ship, only a foot away from my head. All night long they seethed around the *Pequod*, grinding and gnashing at the whale. My dreams were too horrible to describe.

A Barrel of Oil

At last I was to see what the business of whaling was all about. When the sun came up, the whole crew was running across the decks getting the ship ready for our first catch. I stepped over to the bulwarks and had a good look at him, before the day's work began.

From my lessons at school, sailor's stories and pictures in books, I had already formed an idea of the size of a sperm whale. But, in bright sunlight, the animal fixed to the side of the *Pequod* surpassed all my imaginings. He was a breathtaking sight. I paced his length from tip to tail and can vouch he was at least eighty feet long. The tail itself was twenty feet across, I guessed, comprising two huge flukes growing out of the root of his body. His trunk here was only the thickness of a man's waist, quite slender considering his great weight, but after five more paces it thickened into the vast slab of his body, about fourteen feet high. On each side was a short fin, to help him balance and pitch as he swam the world's oceans. Just beyond his fin was the ear and eye, both tiny compared to the rest of his bulk. A sperm whale's eyes are on either side of his massive crown, so he can never look straight ahead – a fact his hunters exploit in the chase. Past his eyes, his head rears up like a battering ram, stretching a full twenty feet or more in length. At his flat brow, no harpoon or knife can mark the iron-hard skin. The head here is solid bone and blubber, smooth as an anvil and twice as tough. A whale's forehead could smash its way through granite if its owner was in that kind of mood. Below the head, set back a good six feet, was the jaw, studded with ivory teeth. The jaw was perhaps fourteen feet long. I shuddered as I thought of my captain watching Moby Dick's crooked jawbone sweeping at him through the foam. On top of the head was a solitary spouting hole, where the whale sucked in air before diving. His lungs had to withstand the incredible pressure of hundreds of tons of water sitting above him, while he pursued his diet of squid at the bottom of the sea.

I marvelled at the sperm whale, and in particular at his noble head. It reminded me of the Bible story about Jonah, the man swallowed by a "great fish" in the Mediterranean. In church, I had found this story hard to believe. But, out here in the middle of the ocean, looking up at the enormous creature before me, I quickly changed my opinion.

Extracting oil from the whale was a crude and violent business. But you must remember we used every drop of this fuel to light our homes and towns, and very little of the whale's body was wasted.

The first step was to fasten two huge hooks to his

blubbery skin, to lift the body out of the water until it was hanging alongside the ship. The masts took the weight of the animal by means of two tackles mounted on them and, as the crew heaved on a rope, the whale was slowly raised. It was such a huge creature, the *Pequod* tilted over by twenty degrees under the burden.

Next, a harpooner made a wide incision in the whale's skin around one of the hooks, and that hook was slowly lowered down to the waves. This was called cutting-in. The weight of the whale's body hanging from the other hook pulled the skin away from his back. With the harpooner slicing and the men raising and lowering the hooks, the whale's blubber was slowly removed in a broad strip, four feet wide and a foot thick. It was a little like peeling an enormous orange. Finally, the strip of whale skin was lowered into a small chamber known as the blubber room.

During this "disrobing" of a sperm whale, sailors would sometimes find whole harpoons embedded in his flesh, corroded and bent with age. Starbuck told me he had once pulled a Native American stone harpoon head from the flukes of an old whale. I wondered about that antique weapon, and what kind of man had thrown it.

When the whale's body was at last stripped bare of its skin and other valuable parts, it was cut through at the base of the head. The hooks were drawn out and the corpse quickly sank below the waves. Only the mighty head remained, hanging from two chains next to the ship's bulwarks. It was about to reveal the most valuable of the leviathan's secrets.

Tashtego swung out onto the whale's lofty crown and cut a hole in the soft blubber around the spout. He dropped a bucket down into this hole, fixed to a length of rope. After fishing around for a moment, he started reeling in the bucket, until it popped out, brimming with a white, frothy liquid. He passed the bucket along a rope to a sailor waiting on deck, and this man poured the precious fluid into a barrel. The operation was repeated eighty or ninety times, until a row of barrels had been filled.

This liquid was spermaceti, the purest of all whale oil, used in the manufacture of fine ointments and candles fit for a cathedral. The sperm whale carried hundred of gallons of it in the reservoir in his head. Why is it, I wondered, that so many valuable things are hidden away in the hardest-to-reach places – diamonds in the hard earth, gold nuggets in mountain riverbeds and oil in a creature that spends most of his life in the depths of the oceans? Men risk their lives to find these things, I told myself. And, just at that moment, I saw one of the chains holding the whale's head twitch and snap apart with an ear-crunching boom. Tashtego lost his footing and tumbled head-first into the hole he had cut in the leviathan's crown.

The sailors on the deck watched in horror as the head quivered and shook with Tashtego's struggles. A second later, the remaining chain made a terrible screeching sound and it too burst apart, sending the head plunging towards the waves. The *Pequod* pitched back from the release of the burden and we were thrown off our feet as the ship rocked back and forth. When I scrambled to the side, I saw the whale's head slipping under the water.

"Man overboard!" screamed a sailor.

A shadow passed over my head and I looked into the sky to see Queequeg, diving into the ocean from the quarterdeck. He had a sharp knife rammed between his teeth.

"Send out a boat," called Starbuck.

I helped two other men launch one of the whaleboats and we rowed over to the spot where the

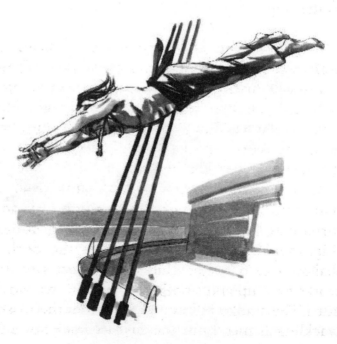

head had disappeared. For a full minute there wasn't any movement on the surface, then I saw a bubble pop up on the surf.

"He's coming," I cried.

An instant later, Queequeg burst out of the water, dragging the stunned Tashtego by the shoulders. When we'd helped them into the boat, my friend explained that he'd managed to cut a hole in the side of the slowly sinking head. He had pulled Tashtego out by the ears, delivering him like a baby.

"There's a message in that," said Starbuck, sitting next to me. "Never give up hope," he whispered, "even when the situation looks hopeless."

I thought I saw him smiling as he ordered us back to the ship.

The last stage of extracting the whale's oil is perhaps the most gruesome. In the middle of the ship is a square, brick hut, measuring ten feet along each wall and standing nearly eight feet high. Hidden inside is a stove. This peculiar construction is known as the try works; in this floating kiln the sailors melt down the whale's blubber into oil.

Under a hatch in the roof of the little brick room stand two iron jugs, or try pots, resting on an iron furnace. To limit the risk of fire spreading around the ship, the furnace is separated from the deck by a shallow tray of water. But, when I first saw the try works fired up and smoking, I was sure we would all burn. The smoke billows up and hides the masts, the crackling flames from the furnace spill out and flit about the deck, and a hellish red glow covers everything in sight.

When the furnace is good and hot, a sailor in the blubber room begins to hack the whale's skin into pillow-sized chunks. These are hauled to the deck, where one of the harpooners scoops them up and flips them into the try pots. They hiss and sizzle, until the oil starts to seep from the blubber. Most of the colossal whale is dropped into those hungry jars, and its oil siphoned away at their base. From there, it is poured into a copper cooling tub. Any residue of bones and ash from the whale skin is scooped out as it rises to the surface, and thrown over the side to the sharks.

Once the oil has cooled to a warm liquid goo, a sailor pours it into great casks hooped with steel rings and rolls them to the lowest part of the ship's hold. The casks are sealed in with timber and tar, and locked away until the ship drops anchor again in her home port.

For a whole day and night, the try works pumped out a foul black smoke, filthy sailors wandered past huge piles of dead whale, and the decks were covered in rusty old casks and pools of blood and oil. It was a scene from an abattoir; noisy, stinking and chaotic. But, a day or two later, the ship was scrubbed clean, the try works' hatches had been screwed firmly in place and the crew had washed themselves from top to toe. It seemed hardly possible that this was the same ship.

Glancing down at the pristine decks, the lookouts in the masts smiled to themselves. At any moment they might sight another whale. Just as the men had finished their spring cleaning, a whale might come along and make them go through the whole back-breaking process all over again.

Such is life on a whaling ship, and such is life itself.

The Grand Armada

The *Pequod* sailed across the Indian Ocean, with her crew scouting for whales in a desert of blue water. We lowered once for an old sperm whale, but as soon as the chase was over and he was dead, his great body started to sink.

"Cut us loose there, Mister Stubb," cried Starbuck. "We don't want to go down with him."

In a matter of seconds our catch had slipped away, heading for the bottom of the ocean. We'd been rowing for hours, and it had been a dangerous hunt, so the loss pained us all.

"There goes a hundred barrels," said Flask bitterly.

"Aye," muttered Stubb. "I wish we could have got him into the pots. I hate to lose a whale."

Most whales float for a day or more when they die, but in rare cases the animal sinks, robbing his hunters of their prize. This stroke of bad luck was keenly felt by the whole crew because we'd only had a few sightings since the last catch. Some of the old whalers told me the hunting in the Indian Ocean had never been worse. Along with the seas off Japan, this was supposed to be one of the world's best whaling grounds. But instead of seeing a group of sperm whales every few hours, as sailors used to do ten years ago, days or weeks could pass without us catching sight of a single animal.

"Have we emptied the seas of whales with all our hunting, first mate?" I asked Starbuck one morning, half-joking. He turned to me and frowned.

"The whale is my livelihood, the means for me to feed my wife and children. Do not laugh about such a thing."

"I am sorry, sir," I responded, feeling a little ashamed.

"And besides," he continued, "there's no shortage of whales in the sea. They've changed their habits, that's all. Now they're hunted, they try to find safety in numbers. They swim in large schools. Only the old bull males swim alone."

"But do you think it's possible we could pose a threat to the existence of the animal?" I asked him. I didn't want to offend him, but here was my chance to learn about the future of the leviathan from one of the most experienced whalers to sail out of Nantucket.

Starbuck stared at me intently. "I do not," he declared in a serious voice. "For three reasons. First, this ship of thirty men might sail around for four years chasing whales, but if we caught only forty of them in all that time, our voyage would be declared a success. That's only ten whales killed each year, lad," he explained, as if doubting my ability in mathematics. "And second, if his numbers decrease, the whale can always hide in the frozen polar seas, where our oars and sails are no use. Lastly, the deep ocean where he swims is as alien and unknown to us as the moon. We could never hunt down every last whale, in all that uncharted water."

"I take your point, sir," I said humbly.

"Don't fear for the whale's survival, Ishmael," the mate concluded. "Fear for your own."

I followed his gaze across the deck to the main mast, where the gold doubloon glittered, and past this to the quarterdeck where our captain stared out to sea, a terrible hunger in his flashing eyes.

But it was too beautiful a morning for me to fret for long over the mate's gloomy words. Starbuck's solid Quaker soul was troubled by the captain's furious quest, but I was here to see the world and study the business of whaling. There was too much worrying in this life, anyway, I decided. My belly was full, I was fit and healthy, and I was out in the balmy tropical seas – these were good enough reasons to be cheerful. I let the mate descend to his airless cabin, while I swung up into the rigging and joined Queequeg to share a joke or two in the sunshine.

It had always been Ahab's intention to steer the *Pequod* past Japan, near the equatorial line that runs across the Pacific Ocean. This was a prime whaling ground where we might fill our hold with oil casks; but it was also the place where our captain's calculations told him he would encounter Moby Dick. So, we cruised to the edge of the Indian

Ocean, making for the Straits of Sunda between the islands of Java and Sumatra. Once through, we'd be able to sail past the Philippines to Japan and beyond.

I rolled out of my hammock one morning and noticed a strange scent on the air. Rushing to the deck, I could see a green smudge on the horizon. After an hour, I saw palm trees and grass-sloped mountain ridges. We were approaching the mouth of the straits. Not for nothing do people call these the spice islands. It was cinnamon I could smell, carried to me on the morning breeze.

"Keep your eyes peeled, men," boomed Ahab to the lookouts. "There are all kinds of monsters in these seas."

"What does he mean?" I asked a passing sailor.

"Piracy," the man whispered, running a finger across his throat as though it were a knife.

"Pirates, out here?" I cried in disbelief.

But, before he could answer, there was a shout from the masts.

"There she blows, a whole armada of them."

I dashed to the side, fearing the worst. A few miles ahead of us, I saw a great semicircle of sperm whales spouting, hundreds of them, moving through the straits.

"Full sail, Mister Starbuck," ordered Ahab. "Let's get after them."

"Captain," came a voice from the rigging. It was Tashtego, pointing to our stern. In the distance, I could see a dozen or so white squares bobbing on the sea.

"Wet the sails," cried Ahab. "A damp sail makes for more speed. And there's a party of Malay pirates chasing after us, lads, just as we chase the whale."

I had read storybook tales of pirates and buccaneers as a boy, but I had thought this breed of men had been driven off the seas a hundred years ago.

"Might they be simple fishermen, captain?" I asked.

"Aye, lad, the kind of fishermen who'll take our ship and throw us to the sharks."

With that, I jumped into the rigging and helped the other sailors wet the sails.

The *Pequod* was old but she was still sprightly. We raced through the straits and into the open sea, leaving the island-hugging pirates shaking their fists in our wake. As soon as Ahab was certain they couldn't follow, he dropped sail.

"Lower the boats," he roared. A minute later I was out of the rigging and pulling with all my might into a great pool of thrashing whales.

Starbuck was right when he guessed that the whales had started swimming together in schools. There was a close-packed field of at least a hundred of them before us. They were moving about in great confusion, beating the water with their fins and tails. Each of the boats struck off, looking for a bull to pick off on the fringes of the armada, and within a few minutes Queequeg had harpooned a large animal. The idea of safety in numbers was a good one, as none of the boats wanted to get too close to the school itself. But as soon as our whale felt the dart biting into his side, he dragged us directly towards them.

Our boat was towed so fast, it cut a white gash through the sea. Queequeg threw the steering oar from side to side, guiding us down narrow channels between angry whales, around their humps and under their flailing tails. He paid special attention to avoiding their tails. The whale's tail is his most dangerous weapon at sea. It rises forty feet above you, blocking out the sun, before smashing down with enough force to turn a whaleboat into sawdust.

At last, the harpoon in our whale slipped out from all his twisting and tugging around the ranks of his comrades, and we glided to a stop right in the heart of the school.

Inside the floating walls of whales, the water was as glassy and smooth as a lake. It was quite a large enclosure, perhaps a square mile of ocean. There was no gap for us to steer through, so we bobbed around examining our prison. I looked over the side of the whaleboat and, to my amazement, realized I was staring straight into the face of a baby whale, or calf, only a few inches below the surface. He was studying me with the same curious expression I imagined must be on my own startled face.

"This has to be the nursery," whispered Queequeg, pointing down to a group of ten or more calves on the other side of the boat, staying close to their mothers.

"No wonder the whales were so agitated," said Starbuck softly. "They were protecting their young."

Suddenly, there was a low hum in the air. The placid waters of our enclosed pond began to bubble and churn. A great bull whale crashed towards us, perhaps fleeing from one of the other boats, and his excitement panicked the other animals.

"To your oars," hissed Starbuck, still trying not to speak too loudly and alarm the whales closest to us. Then, with a sound like ice cracking in a frozen river, the whales began sliding over each other, rolling and thrashing in fear. Our lake of calm water shrank until the whales were pressing in on us. We rowed for all we were worth, darting between their huge shapes and ducking when a sweeping tail came too close. At last, we were out in open water, rushing back to the other boats. Flask had killed a whale and was towing it back to the ship. Stubb had hooked one but it had escaped him. He was empty-handed, as were we.

"The more whales you see before you," coughed the disgruntled mate, "the fewer you catch."

Ambergris

I have mentioned the sweet scent of cinnamon that came wafting across the decks of the *Pequod* as we passed close to one of the spice islands. A week or two after we met the great armada of whales, another aroma, just as strong, drifted around the ship. But this smell was more of a stench than a perfume; it was a flat, reeking stink that made the sailors pinch their noses.

"Ship ahoy," came the lookout's call. "It's fixed to a blasted whale."

I could see a whaling ship ahead of us, with the carcass of a leviathan hanging from its side. A "blasted" whale is one that's died from natural causes or an old wound, and been found floating on the ocean in a state of decay. This explained the terrible gas that was enveloping us – a whale that's been dead for two days or more gives off a smell bad enough to make the masts wilt.

"She's a Frenchy," cried Stubb, who was studying the other ship through a telescope. "And I'll bet my hammock that she's picked up the whale I lost from that school. That's my harpoon sticking out there,

I'm sure of it."

As we approached the ship I saw a second whale, chained to the starboard side. It was a strange, shrivelled animal, old and withered, and it gave off a smell that was even worse than the first. The sight made Stubb rub his hands with excitement.

"She's got a dry one too," he yelled. "I wonder if she knows what to do with it, or if she's planning to melt some oil."

"There's more oil in my boot leather than there is in that whale," said Flask in disgust.

"You're right," answered Stubb. "But she might hide other riches. Boat crew on deck," he ordered.

I had come across tales of dry whales in the course of my reading. They were animals that had passed away from some unknown, ravaging disease. But I had no idea what riches could be found in them, or what Stubb was hinting at. I was immediately curious and wanted to learn more.

As luck would have it, during the last violent lowering in Stubb's boat, one of his crew had torn the muscles in his arm. I volunteered to take his place, as I knew he was still in some pain, and he was happy to give up his seat. A moment later, I was rowing towards the French ship.

When we were close enough, I could see that the thick, curving timber used to shape the prow was carved into a drooping stalk. It was painted green and, for thorns, it had copper spikes poking out of it.

At the top was a bright red bulb of wood.

"She's the *Bouton de Rose*," shouted one of the men, making out her nameplate.

"The *Rosebud* eh?" laughed Stubb. "I'd guessed it already from the carving. Don't she smell like a petal? Ahoy there, *Bouton de Rose*, are there any of you rosebuds that speak English?"

"There are," answered a burly man from up on the deck. "But I'm the only one. First mate, at your service."

"Have you seen the White Whale, Rosie?" called Stubb, chuckling through his fingers. We were covering our noses with our hands, against the awful stench.

"Never heard of it," replied the mate.

"Hold fast then," Stubb cried. "I'll be back in a minute."

We left the mate looking baffled and returned to the *Pequod*. Ahab was waiting on the quarterdeck for our report.

"The answer's no, sir," called Stubb. Our captain shook his head and stormed off across the deck, while we rowed back to the *Rosebud* and her smelly cargo. The mate was getting ready to cut into the whale with a long spade, and had fitted a canvas sack over his nose.

"What's wrong with your sniffer," called Stubb, "is it broken?"

"I wish it was," grunted the man. "I'd be better off without it."

"Now you mention it," joked Stubb, "there is a

whiff in the air. You couldn't throw us down some rose petals to take our minds off it could you?"

The mate flew into a fury. "What's your business here?"

"I'm trying to give you some friendly advice," Stubb cooed. "You should know it's fool's work trying to get oil out of whales like these. That dried-up one doesn't have a glassful in his whole carcass."

"Do you think I don't know that?" replied the mate, looking exasperated. "I've had this smell in my nostrils for the last three days, knowing full well the whales are worthless. But this is my captain's first voyage and he won't listen to me. I wonder," said the man, scratching his blanketed nose, "perhaps he'd listen to you. Would you come aboard and speak with him?"

"I'd do anything to help a fellow whaler in distress," answered Stubb cunningly. He scrambled up the boarding nets and joined the other mate on deck. But, before he could speak, there was a crash from the roundhouse cabin at the far end of the ship and a man ran out and shouted at the mate in French. When he had finished, he clapped his hand over his nose and ran back into the roundhouse.

"That's the ship's surgeon," the mate said calmly. "He says he's told the captain we're all going to get the plague because of the gas from the whales, but he still won't listen."

"Oh dear," responded Stubb with a sneer. "But are you really the only man here who speaks English?"

"I am."

"Then how am I to chat with your captain?"

"You could let me do the talking," answered the mate, looking as sly as Stubb. "The last thing in the world I want to be doing today is boiling up these smelly, dried-out whales. If you let me pretend to interpret for you, I'll convince the captain we should get rid of them."

"But what do I say for you to translate?" asked Stubb.

"Anything you want."

Stubb smiled. "Let's go down to his cabin, friend," he chortled. "I like your plan."

Before they'd taken a step, a nervous-looking man in elaborate dress had popped out of the roundhouse. It was the captain. He darted over to his mate and looked Stubb up and down.

"What shall we say to him, then?" the mate asked Stubb.

Stubb, looking impish, could hardly keep himself from chuckling. "Tell him I think he looks a little overdressed to be a sailor. Where's his top hat?"

The first mate turned to the captain and let out a stream of French. Leaning forward in the whaleboat I could hear him clearly, and having worked hard at school I could understand most of what he was saying. I translated it back to my huddle of friends in the boat.

"He says," I began, "that yesterday, this man, he means Stubb, met a ship whose captain, first mate and six sailors had all died from a fever, caught from a blasted whale."

The captain's face turned white and his eyes rolled back in his head.

"Anything else?" the mate asked Stubb. "I think it's working," he added.

"Tell him he's an overdressed baboon," Stubb responded. "He looks as though he's going to a dinner dance, not roving the oceans looking for man-eating whales."

"This man tells me," said the mate earnestly to his frightened captain, "that the gas from the dried whale is twice as deadly as the other. He says that if we value our lives, we must cut loose both whales at once."

The captain rushed over and shouted to the sailors down in the forecastle. In a second, a dozen men ran up to the deck and crowded around the chains fastening the whales, making ready to drop them back into the sea.

"Is that all?" the mate asked Stubb, with a barely concealed smile. His plan had worked out perfectly.

"Tell him he's been diddled," said Stubb. Then, turning to us sailors in the boat, he mouthed the words, "and he's not the only one."

The mate was too busy speaking with his captain to notice Stubb's trickery. "Once the whales are cut free," he was explaining, "we must lower our boats and tow the ship away from them. There's not enough wind to fill the sails and it's urgent that we escape the poisonous gas coming from the carcasses."

The mate was so sick of the smell that he wasn't content with letting the animals drift away slowly. He wanted to find some clean air.

"Could I be of any help?" interrupted Stubb. He had guessed what the mate was saying and was rubbing his hands in excitement. "My boat could pull the dry whale, which is the lighter of the two bodies, away from your own ship."

The mate translated and the captain shook Stubb's hand and thanked him. Before we knew what was happening, Stubb was back in our whaleboat and had thrown a line to one of the *Rosebud's* crew. The obliging sailor fastened it around the whale and we started tugging and heaving at the oars.

"She's moving, lads," Stubb yelled. "No slacking. Put your backs into it now."

He steered us over to the far side of the *Pequod*, and as soon as we were out of sight of the grateful *Rosebud*, ordered us to lift oars.

"Let's get next to her," he said, lifting the line and starting to haul it in.

"But the smell, sir," I protested.

"Breath through your mouth if you're the sensitive type," he barked at me. "Pass me that boat spade."

We were alongside the dry whale now, close enough for Stubb to touch its skin. I watched in horror as he made an incision with the boat spade just behind the fin, then shoved his hands into the corpse, right up to his elbows.

"It should be right about here," he called back to us. For five minutes he felt around inside the whale, and the stench grew worse with every minute. At last he began to curse, and I thought he was about to give up, but then I noticed a sweet scent mingling with the foul smell already in the air.

"That's it," he called in triumph. "I knew we'd find some."

He pulled out his cupped hands. They were loaded with a yellow, waxy substance that looked like a crushed bar of soap.

"Ambergris, lads," hissed Stubb. "Worth its weight in gold to a perfume maker. Pass me a sack."

We helped him scrape six handfuls of the precious substance from the cavity in the whale.

"Nobody knows," he told us, "whether it's ambergris that causes the illness that kills the whale, or if ambergris itself is produced by the illness. But it's used by kings and queens as a base for their scents, and I bet they've never guessed its origin – the rotten belly of a sickly whale."

"Stubb," we heard Ahab roaring from the quarterdeck, "get back here. The wind's up and I want to make sail."

"Blast the old man," muttered Stubb. "We could have got a handful or two more, I reckon. But we'll have to leave it to the sharks. Row us back lads. But remember, if a rich landlubber ever strolls up and tells you whaling men and their whales all smell like a sewer, he could well be wearing ambergris perfume rubbed behind his ears."

On the Samuel Enderby

We were making good progress towards the Sea of Japan when we sighted another whaling ship, the *Samuel Enderby*, coming up on our port side. Ahab jumped into his hoisted whaling boat as the other ship closed on us.

"Have you seen the White Whale?" he called across the waves.

The other captain was a stout, good-natured looking Englishman of about sixty, well-tanned, with a fine, blue uniform.

"Have you seen this?" he yelled back to Ahab, holding up a stump of whale bone where his arm should have been. At the end of the ivory limb, instead of fingers, there was a hammer head, carved out of the bone.

"Stubb," commanded Ahab, "call your crew and take me over there."

We rowed out across a calm sea. When we reached the *Samuel Enderby*, I realized Ahab might have some problem getting aboard. On the *Pequod*, he had a special pulley with a plank as a seat, to hoist him up to the deck, but the English ship only had a rope

ladder hanging over her side. The smiling captain standing above us saw the difficulty at once.

"Lower the cutting hook," he told his men. "And bring one of his crew aboard to aid him."

We watched the huge blubber hook being winched down to us, and Ahab slid his good leg into its curve. A moment later he was standing next to the English captain, and I was being lifted to join him.

"Let us shake bones together," roared Ahab, as soon as he got his balance. He lifted his ivory leg and knocked it against the Englishman's false arm. Rather than looking surprised, the captain laughed heartily, obviously enjoying the bone handshake.

"Now... the White Whale," hissed Ahab, "where and when did you see it?"

The Englishman lifted his white arm and pointed

out to sea. "Out on the Pacific Equator line, last season."

"And he took your arm off?"

"I hold him responsible for it. Did he take that leg of yours?"

"Never mind that," Ahab snapped impatiently. "Tell me your story."

"Very well," said the captain, with a wry smile. "It was my first cruise along the equator and I'd just hooked a handsome sperm whale. I had him on a line of rope from my whaleboat. He was a big brute, and was pulling me around like a circus horse pulls a clown, when a whale twice his size pops up from the bottom of the sea."

"How did he look?" hissed Ahab.

"He had a milky-white head and a wrinkled hump."

"That's him," said Ahab, his eyes flashing. "Go on."

"I remember, there was a harpoon sticking out near his starboard fin."

"That was my harpoon," Ahab interrupted. "And then?"

"I'll tell the story if you'll give me a chance," said the Englishman, with a wry smile. "This whale you're so interested in took a hold of my harpoon line and bit it in two. Then he sounded, the other whale swam off and we were left empty-handed. I ordered my men to haul the line in, but the frayed ends of it must have caught in the white whale's teeth. Before we knew it, he'd surfaced and we were beached on his snowy hump."

"He's devilish cunning," muttered Ahab to himself.

"Seeing that this whale had deprived me of my catch, and seeing he was the biggest and most noble sperm whale I'd ever come across, I resolved to capture him. So, I hopped into my first mate's boat which was right alongside mine, grabbed a harpoon and sank it deep into the white monster's hide. The next instant I was blinded with salt water as he thrashed around in a rage. When I'd rubbed my eyes clear, I saw his tail towering above me like a marble steeple. It came crashing down on my boat. The craft was broken in two and the whale flailed around trying to crush us. I caught hold of my harpoon, still firm in his side, and stuck to him like one of those pilot fish that nibbles around a shark for scraps. But he dived underwater and shook me off. I thought that was the last I'd see of him, but the next second I was sucked under the waves, caught on a stray lance that was trailing from his side. Its barb sank into my shoulder and I was towed down behind him. Just as I thought my lungs were about to crack, and I would have to follow that terrible white shadow down into the depths, the blade slipped along my arm and came out at the wrist."

"A shocking bad wound," said a stately-looking gentleman stepping up onto the quarterdeck. "I am the ship's surgeon who treated Captain Boomer's injuries. Despite my careful attentions..."

"Pouring rum down my throat," interrupted Boomer. "And down his own at the same time."

"I sat with him every night for weeks," the doctor added, looking hurt by his captain's remark.

"As a drinking companion," laughed Boomer.

"Now really," said the doctor, "I am an abstinent man. I never drink..."

"Water," interrupted the captain with a chortle. "He never touches it. Only takes rum. But I don't mean to offend, sir. Please finish the story."

"I may as well," the doctor said coolly. "The wound was almost three feet long and it refused to heal. When it began to turn black I had no choice. Off came the arm. But this ivory limb was nothing to do with me. The captain ordered the carpenter to make it, and insisted on that violent-looking hammer in place of a hand."

"But what happened to the White Whale?" Ahab demanded, growing frustrated with the Englishmen's banter.

"He sounded," said Boomer, "and I went back to my ship, before I bled to death. It was only a month later I heard talk of Moby Dick, and then I knew who it was that had taken my arm."

"Have you seen him since?"

"Twice."

"But you couldn't get a harpoon into him?" asked Ahab, looking confused.

"I didn't try," said Boomer softly. "Isn't the loss of one limb hard enough to bear? He's welcome to my arm, since there's nothing I can do to get it back. But I won't risk the other. No more tussles with Moby Dick for me, no sir. There would be great glory in killing him," he admitted, nodding his head, "and there's a shipload of precious sperm oil in him, of that I'm sure. But he's best left alone. Don't you think so, captain?" he asked, glancing down at Ahab's ivory leg.

"He is," replied Ahab. "But he will still be hunted. He is like a magnet to me, and I will chase him off the edge of this world if I have to. When did you see him last? Where was he heading?"

"Bless my soul," cried the surgeon. "Are you fevered, sir? Your blood is almost boiling. Let me examine you."

He stepped close to Ahab, ready to take hold of his wrist and check the pulse.

"Avast," roared Ahab, shoving the doctor away from him. "Back to the boat, Ishmael. Boomer, which way was he heading?"

"Good God," cried the English captain, "what's the matter with you? He was heading east, I think. Is your captain crazy?" he whispered to me.

"Take me down," Ahab ordered, and he was hastily lowered back to our boat. In vain, the English captain hailed him across the water.

"Don't do it, man. There's no comfort for the vengeful, only more sorrows ahead."

Ahab stood upright as we rowed, ignoring the shouts. He turned his back on the *Samuel Enderby* and set his face like flint, staring directly ahead.

Queequeg Orders a Coffin

We cut a wake through the pearl-smooth waters of the South China Sea, always advancing on the Pacific's equatorial whaling grounds. This was where Ahab had met Moby Dick the year before and where he hoped to meet him again.

When our captain wasn't grinding away at his mooring hole lookout, he was down in his cabin, studying his charts. I was scrubbing the floor of the cramped hallway outside his quarters one morning, when Starbuck rushed past me with an alarmed expression on his face. He knocked on Ahab's door and, when there was no response, stepped in, leaving the door ajar behind him. I was especially diligent washing the patch of floor just around my captain's cabin – after all, I had a duty to keep my friends in the forecastle informed of any important news.

I peered in and had a quick look around the private temple that was the captain's cabin. It was neat and unremarkable, lined with bookshelves, a rack of firearms, and a glass cabinet containing bottles and scientific instruments. Then I noticed Ahab's unmade bed in the corner of the room. The sheets were all knotted and thrown about, as though a wild animal had slept there. When I asked the steward about this later, he told me the captain never went into a truly deep sleep. He always thrashed around like an angry whale for an hour or two, trying to drift off, before jumping up again and shouting for his clothes.

The charts spread across Ahab's table were almost as jumbled as his bedding. With his white peg braced against the table, my captain was leaning over and tracing a course on a map detailing the coast of Japan. He was so involved in his navigational work that he didn't look up until the first mate cleared his throat.

"Get back on deck," growled Ahab. "Can't you see I'm busy?"

"The oil in the hold is leaking out, sir," Starbuck said boldly. "We were drenching the casks with water to keep the wood supple, and found oil mingled in with it. There's a leak. We must open the hold, sir, and bring the barrels up for checks."

"Open the hold?" roared Ahab, slamming his fist down on the sea chart. "Waste a week checking barrels when we're almost off Japan?"

"Either that, or waste in one day more oil than we might get in a year. What we've voyaged thousands of miles to catch is worth the effort, sir."

"So it is," replied Ahab, staring at the chart moodily, "if we get him in the end."

"I was speaking of the oil in the hold, sir," said Starbuck abruptly.

"But I wasn't," snapped Ahab. "Now return to the

deck. Let it all leak out."

"What will the ship's owners say, sir?" asked Starbuck in dismay.

"What do I care about them? The only master you have to worry about is the master of this ship – Ahab. Now get back on deck."

"Captain," said the mate, his face reddening with rage and frustration, "you are testing me to my limits, sir."

"You dare to criticize me?" cried Ahab, raising himself to his full, imposing height.

"I dare to be troubled about this voyage, sir. I have a duty to the good of this ship and its mission."

Ahab seized a musket from the rack of firearms on the wall. He lifted its muzzle close to Starbuck's chest. "There is one God who is Lord over the Earth," he hissed "and one captain that is Lord over the *Pequod*. Now get back on deck."

I could see Starbuck clenching his fists and trying to control himself. Then he stepped back to the hall, pausing an instant in the doorway.

"I am not insulted, but amazed by you, captain," he said calmly. "I know my duty and I fear for this ship. But I tell you not to beware of your first mate. No, beware of Ahab, I say. Beware of yourself, old man." He turned and hurried past me along the gangway.

"Ahab, beware of Ahab," I heard my captain mutter to himself. "He has a point there." He paced around in the cabin for a moment and then made his way up to the deck. I couldn't resist following him.

"Starbuck, a word with you," Ahab called across

the boards. "You are too good a man, mate, that's your problem. Empty the main hold and find that leak for me."

I don't know if Ahab had suffered a pang of guilt about the proper duty of a captain to his employers, or if it was a tactical decision to ensure his first mate's loyalty. But, an hour later, the decks of the *Pequod* were covered in barrels, steel hoops, piles of timber and everything else we carried. The decks knocked like a hollow log as the men ran about over the empty hold and the ship rolled heavily despite the calm sea. It was a good job a storm didn't blow up then — we were so top-heavy that we would have quickly capsized.

Poor Queequeg was given the task of checking the barrels on the very floor of the hold. It was a dirty job, crawling around in that dampness and slime, and with all his tattoos he looked like a green lizard sitting at the bottom of a well. At last he detected the leaky barrel, which was brought up and repaired. But the chill, fuggy atmosphere gave Queequeg a sniffle, and then a cold. This developed into a fever and, within a day or two, he was stretched out in his hammock, close to death.

I stayed by his side as much as I could. His powerful physique wasted away and his bones began to jab through his painted skin. Only his eyes refused to surrender to the disease; they grew brighter even as his body became too weak to lift his head from the pillow.

"When a whaler dies in Nantucket," he whispered to mc, "they lay him in a long box that looks like a canoe."

For a moment I was confused, and then I realized he must be describing a coffin.

"This reminds me of the custom on my own island," he went on. "They place a dead warrior in his canoe and float him out to sea. Where the edge of the ocean joins the sky, that is where he sails."

He grasped my hand with the little strength he had left. "I don't want to be fed to the sharks," he cried. "Build me one of the canoes I have seen."

I ran down to see the ship's carpenter and told him of my friend's last request. The grizzled old man didn't blink an eye at the order. He rummaged around in some of the lumber that had come out of the darkest recesses of the hold. After selecting some sturdy, ebony planks, he visited Queequeg to get his measurements.

For an hour or two I could hear the carpenter hammering and sawing at his work bench on the deck above us. Then he appeared at the hatch to the forecastle with the coffin balanced across his shoulder.

"Is it needed yet?" he called.

"It is not," I shouted back in anger. But Queequeg managed to roll over in his hammock.

"Bring it to me," he whispered.

When the coffin was lying next to his hammock, Queequeg stared at it for a good ten minutes.

"My harpoon," he muttered at last. "Ishmael, place the blade head and a paddle in the canoe. Then bring biscuits, a flask of water and a bag of earth scraped up from the hold. Arrange them inside."

When this was all done he asked me to lay him out in the box.

"Lift the hatch," he whispered.

The carpenter had put a hinge in the lid so the section over the head could be tied open. Queequeg lay there a moment with his body covered, staring up at me with sad eyes.

"Bring Yojo," he asked.

He stood the little idol on his chest and we were silent.

"It'll do," he said softly, and the sick man was carried back to his hammock.

But, now that he had made every preparation for death and checked his coffin was a good fit, Queequeg changed his mind about going anywhere.

"I can't die yet," he told me one morning. "I've

remembered there's something I have to attend to on my island first."

Already the blood was coming back into his face, and his skin was looking healthier.

"Queequeg," I said in amazement, "can you really choose whether you live or die?"

"Of course," he said with a smile. "Only a whale, or a gale, or some outside destroyer can kill a man if he's made up his mind he wants to live. Sickness alone cannot do it."

For three days he lounged around the decks, regaining his strength. On the fourth day, he stretched his limbs, yawned and shook his head.

"I am fit again," he declared. He had thrown off a tropical fever that would have killed most men. His convalescence was completed in less than a week. Having cheated death, my friend put the coffin he'd ordered to good use.

He used it as a sea chest.

The Forge

The *Pequod* had its own blacksmith as well as a carpenter. His name was Perch and he was great, hulking man with bloodshot eyes. He wore a matted beard, and his skin was blistered and scarred from a lifetime of working red-hot metals. His forge and anvil were bolted to the deck just by the main mast, and he prowled around the burning coals in a shiny, sharkskin apron.

When the *Pequod* finally slipped into the Pacific Ocean, I stared into its thousand shades of blue, rippling all the way to the Galapagos Islands and the west coast of the Americas. It fascinated me. But Ahab was unimpressed. He was only interested in visiting the blacksmith. The crew looked at the Pacific from the bulwarks and saw the Earth's largest body of water, a thing of wonder, home to scattered coral islands and exotic peoples. Ahab glanced over the side and crunched his lips together like the jaws of a vice, until the lines on his forehead stood out. He saw nothing there but a watery battlefield – the territory of his enemy, Moby Dick. He pushed past us, carrying a small leather bag under one arm.

Perch was beating a glowing strip of iron on his anvil and the sparks were flying with each blow from his hammer.

"Blacksmith," cried Ahab. "You live among the sparks, but they don't scorch you. How is that?"

"Because I am already scorched all over, Captain Ahab," answered Perch. "You can't scorch a scar."

"What is it you're working on?" asked Ahab.

"An old boat-spade, sir. It had some dents in it."

"Can you make it smooth again?"

"I think so, sir," replied Perch.

"Can you smooth any dents, never mind how hard the metal is, blacksmith?" said Ahab craftily.

"All dents but one," answered Perch.

"Look here, then," cried Ahab, stepping forward and beating his own lined forehead with a fist. "Can you smooth my maddened brow? I'll gladly lay my head on your anvil and feel your hammer blows rain between my eyes if you can smooth that out."

"That is the one I cannot mend, sir," said Perch sadly. "There I cannot help you."

"Then help me with this," said Ahab, jingling the leather bag as if it was full of coins. "I want you to make me a harpoon, Perch, with a blade so strong and sharp that it will stick in the side of the leviathan like his own fin-bone, and take the strain of a thousand whales pulling on it."

"What's in your bag, captain?" whispered Perch curiously.

"These are the stubs from the steel shoes of race horses."

"Horseshoe nails?" Perch gasped. "That's the hardest metal we blacksmiths ever forge, sir."

"Weld them together like glue," hissed Ahab. "Make twelve rods, and then wind and twist and hammer those rods into one shaft, so I know it will never snap. Quick, I'll work the fire for you."

Perch started beating and working the metal, until all twelve rods were ready. Ahab insisted on checking each one, making the smith work them over if he detected any flaw. Then Ahab took the hammer and Perch fed the rods into the forge. When they were white-hot, the smith passed them to his captain and Ahab pounded them together on the anvil.

The sun was slipping into the sea now, and as I watched the two men working like devilish shadows at the mast, I saw Fedallah appear in the gloom. He glided across the deck and stood by the fire, his lips moving as if he was uttering some curse or blessing. When Ahab looked up at his sinister assistant, Fedallah slipped back into the darkness.

"Now for the blade head," yelled Ahab. "Here are my razors, Perch, made of the finest steel. Melt them down and make me some barbs as sharp as fangs."

"Captain," asked Perch nervously, "is this harpoon intended for the White Whale?"

"It is," roared Ahab. "Forge me a blade that will slice right through him."

Perch did as he was commanded, and welded a steel blade shaped like a large arrowhead onto the shaft of the harpoon.

"Pass me the water bucket, sir. I must temper the steel."

"Stop," cried Ahab, snatching the glowing rod from the smith. "I want no ordinary water to baptize my harpoon. Ahoy there, Queequeg, Daggoo and Tashtego, will you step forward? Will you give me enough of your pagan blood to cover this fiery blade?"

The three men nodded and stepped over to their captain. They made cuts in their arms and filled a cup with their shared blood. Ahab lowered the red-hot steel into it, until it spluttered and smoked.

"May the Devil bless you," he howled, lifting the harpoon into the night air. "Carpenter, fetch me a length of hickory," he ordered. "And a coil of towline."

We sailors looked on in disbelief as our captain tied a thirty foot length of rope between the mast and one of the winches on the quarterdeck. He stretched the line taut and then checked every inch of it for signs of fraying or wear. When he was satisfied that the rope was of the finest quality, he unravelled a few inches of one end of it and braided these around the socket of his harpoon. Then he hammered the wooden pole onto the socket, so the rope was fastened tight inside and couldn't be pulled out unless the steel itself split open. Finally, he coiled the trailing rope around his arm and marched off to his cabin, the sound of his ivory leg and the hickory pole tapping on every plank and echoing off into the deep.

Some sailors say that sounds travel for hundred of miles under the ocean. As I watched my captain storm off with his weapon, I wondered if Moby Dick himself might have heard his knocking.

Four Prophecies

Sailing deeper into the teeming Japanese whaling grounds, the *Pequod* was soon busy catching whales. I had never worked so hard in all my life. For hours on end I was out in the boats, rowing until my hands were so stiff that I couldn't straighten my fingers.

When we caught a leviathan on a harpoon, we were sometimes dragged all over the ocean on what sailors call a Nantucket Sleigh Ride. A whale could pull us four or five miles from the ship before he was exhausted. There was nothing to do but grip the oar locks and try to enjoy the ride. Rowing back with the dead whale could take us half a day or more, and we still had to fasten on the chains and secure him to the ship before we could finally climb into our hammocks to rest.

Other whales sounded as soon as we harpooned them. Their flukes would rise up to the clouds and then plunge straight down, sinking so fast that the line would smoke as it flew over the prow of the boat. Every man watched the emptying line tub, waiting to see if we would have to fix another rope to the end of the first. We only carried two line tubs, and there were some whales who dived so deep, they took us to the last few turns of twine. I'd heard stories of boats and their crews that vanished from the sea, yanked down in a flash by a diving whale. The mate waited with his axe poised on the line, ready to slice through it at the last second. Then, suddenly, the rope would go slack and coils of it would bob up around our keel. In those moments before the whale surfaced, I could feel every drop of sweat trickling down my back. I had never forgotten the Manxman's story of the ramming.

But the beauty of the Pacific was enough to make up for all the hard work and the danger we faced every day. Each morning the sun came up and cast a golden light over the water. The waves resembled a summer prairie, their rolling crests like a tall, lush grass blown softly by the breeze.

In these rich seas, other ships had filled their holds with oil and were already making for home. While we pushed deeper into the Pacific, and towards the lair of the White Whale, the Nantucket whaler *Bachelor* sailed past us on the wind, bound for America.

Before we even sighted her sails, we could hear the thud of drums and music carried ahead of her on the wind. Three of her men were up in the high rigging, playing fiddles made of whale bone, while the try pots had been covered in the leviathan's skin and the mates beat out a drunken rhythm on them with their harpoon poles. As the ship came closer, we saw bunting and streamers flying. A sailor had hoisted all their signal flags and ensigns to make the *Bachelor's* masts look like the boughs of a well-decorated Christmas tree. There were casks and bottles full of oil hanging up there too. Indeed, every inch of the ship seemed to be covered in barrels and containers of all sizes and designs.

Starbuck hailed one of the *Bachelor's* mates, who explained the situation. The *Bachelor's* decks were flooded with sperm oil. They'd been so lucky with their catches, the carpenter had run out of barrels to store the melted oil and he'd had to buy more from other ships encountered on the waves. The sailors had even caulked and pitched their sea chests with tar. This process of filling all the cracks and protecting the wood made the chests watertight, so they could be filled with the precious liquid from the whale. All the spare timber had been shaped into barrels; even the captain's dining table had been broken down. He ate his meals off an upturned cask of oil with a tablecloth spread across it.

Groups of sailors were glugging rum and singing in the rigging, while the mates and the harpooners stayed down on the main deck, dancing with the Polynesian girls who had eloped with them earlier in their bountiful voyage.

The captain was alone on his quarterdeck, looking down at his happy crew and enjoying every second of the celebrations.

"Come aboard," he called to Ahab, with a broad, welcoming smile. "I have some good wine in my cabin. It's the only bottle on my ship that isn't full of sperm oil."

"Have you seen the White Whale?" Ahab shouted, ignoring the invitation.

"No," he replied, "only heard talk of him. But I don't believe he exists."

"You're too jolly for me," cried Ahab sourly. "Sail on."

"Come aboard," the other captain tried again. "I'll soon take that frown off your face."

"No," called Ahab, "you're a full ship and homeward bound. I'm an empty ship and outward-bound. We must go our separate ways. Starbuck, steer to the east."

As the two vessels parted, the crew of the *Pequod* looked on enviously at the cheery *Bachelor*.

If you spend time with lucky people, it sometimes happens that some of their luck will rub off on you. The day after we met the happy *Bachelor*, we sighted whales and killed four of them – one for each boat we launched.

Because I was on lookout duty when the first whales were sighted, Starbuck had asked Ahab for the loan of one of his crew. But when more whales were spotted, Ahab ordered me out of the rigging and I hurried down to join his boat.

It was getting late when our whale finally went into his flurry – the last, frenzied thrashings before death. The sun had set and it was too dark to see the ship, so Ahab mounted a lantern on the whale's back and moored his boat along its side.

"We'll find them at dawn," he whispered, pulling his heavy coat around his ears and lying back in the prow.

I tried to sleep, but the planks dug into my back and because I'd neglected to bring a hat with me that afternoon, my cheeks were sun-scorched and itchy. When I leaned over the side to splash my face with water, I saw a shark glide by, his pale skin spectral in the lantern's flickering beam. Then I saw a pack of them, gnawing at the dead whale. I looked along the boat and saw that I wasn't the only man still awake. Fedallah was sitting up with his arms crossed, gazing down at the feeding sharks. Their tails slapped the thin boards of our boat, and Ahab suddenly reared up, startled and moaning.

"I have dreamed it again," he gasped.

"Of hearses?" Fedallah replied in a hiss, not turning to look at his captain. "But I have already told you, Ahab, neither hearse nor coffin will be yours."

"So, I am to die at sea," Ahab muttered to himself. "No drowned man rides in a hearse."

"But before you can die," Fedallah continued, never taking his eyes from the lunging jaws of the sharks, "you must see two hearses riding on the waves. The first is not made by mortal hands and the second is built of wood, grown in your own country."

"That's a strange vision, Fedallah. I can't believe we'll see any hearses out here," said Ahab, much relieved.

"Believe what you want. You cannot die until you see them."

"Is there more?" asked Ahab. "What else have you seen?"

"I will go before you," replied Fedallah.

"You have witnessed your own death?" asked Ahab, his eyes wide in horror.

"And I will appear before you, after my death, to act as your pilot."

"But how can that be?" cried Ahab, clapping his hands together in his excitement. "The sea doesn't give up its dead. If you are right, I must die on land. That means no whale can kill me."

"Only rope can kill you, captain," Fedallah whispered.

"A hangman's rope, you mean? Then I am immortal," laughed Ahab, "immortal on land and on sea."

After this, the two men were silent. In the eerie light from the lantern, they looked like ragged survivors, huddled together after a devastating flood.

I pretended to be asleep until dawn came. Then we rowed until noon to reach the side of the ship.

Typhoon

The most beautiful things can also be the most deadly. I had never seen a sea so tranquil and serene as the Pacific on a good day. But these soothing waters were also home to the fiercest storms of all – the typhoons. They can burst out of a cloudless sky in a matter of minutes, exploding like a bomb over the ocean.

From the main deck of the *Pequod* I watched the sky ahead of us turn green, then brown, then black. It was only early afternoon but the sun dimmed and vanished, while the sea began to swell and foam in anticipation of what was to come. A sudden streak of lightning tore through the air and the following crack was so loud it sounded as if the sky itself was splitting apart.

"Lash your boats down," yelled Stubb.

I sprinted over to help another sailor secure our boat, but before we had the ropes tight, a wind hit the prow of the *Pequod* and knocked us off our feet. It flipped our boat over and slammed it into the bulwarks.

"Hurry up there. Bring in the sails," Starbuck

called to the men in the rigging. But he was already too late.

Peering up into what was now a night sky, it was so dark, I saw one of the main sails torn from a mast, flap out to sea and land in the waves. As I watched, the other masts were stripped too, leaving only a few rags fluttering in their place.

"Mind that boat," the first mate called to me. I jumped up and managed to rope the swaying hull of our whaleboat to a fixing peg, then ran across to help the other sailors. All the boats were quickly lashed down, except Ahab's, which was winched up above the quarterdeck and already tied into position. We thought it was safe, but an enormous wave rushed along the side of the ship and surged up into the stern of the suspended boat. It left a hole big enough for a man to slip through in her bottom.

"Look where this storm comes from," cried Starbuck to Stubb. "It's on the same course he ordered me to steer to find his cursed White Whale."

"You're too gloomy and serious, sir," answered Stubb. "You see sinister meanings in every insignificant thing."

"But look where the largest wave struck us. Right in the place where our captain stands. I wish we could use this wind to blow us all the way back to Nantucket."

The sky was so dark now that it was impossible to see one side of the ship from the other. Only when the lightning crackled could I tell where I was going in all the gloom and black spray from the waves. Just as a great white fork of lightning flashed across the deck, I saw Ahab groping his way along the bulwarks towards his mooring hole.

"The rods, men," cried Starbuck, suddenly remembering his duty to the ship. "Are they overboard yet?"

On every high church tower or cathedral spire on land, a lightning rod runs down into the earth to divert the force of a strike. Ships use a similar tool, a chain fixed to a rod that is strapped to the main mast. The chain has to be much deeper than any part of the hull and this creates quite a drag through the water. For that reason, the lower part of it is stored on deck in fair weather. It is only thrown overboard if a storm blows up.

"Blast the rods," yelled Ahab into the wind. "I don't fear this storm. We'll sail right through it, Starbuck."

But Starbuck wasn't listening to his captain. He was staring up at the masts and the yardarms that hold the sails in place. They were coated in white flames, crackling and humming all around the woodwork.

"Have mercy on us," I heard Stubb cry out in terror. "The masts are ablaze."

The rest of the crew were silent, frozen where they stood, gazing up at the glowing masts. It was hypnotic and terrifying, this apparition around the high parts of the ship. I had heard stories of it appearing on doomed vessels at sea, but I had never believed they were true. It is known as St. Elmo's Fire, after St. Elmo, the patron saint of sailors. I guessed it had something to do with the lightning and other strange forces swirling in the air around our ship. But it was hard not to imagine an evil hand closing in on the *Pequod*, ready to crush us at any second.

As suddenly as it had appeared on the masts, the white fire vanished. The crew stared at each other in wonder and Starbuck crossed the deck to the second mate.

"Do you still think I'm imagining things, Stubb? I heard you cry out for mercy."

"Oh no, that wasn't it," replied Stubb, trying to hide his fear. "I was blessing the fire. The masts reminded me of three huge candles, and I took it as a good omen. We'll fill the hold with so much oil, it will seep into the masts and turn them into spermaceti candles."

Starbuck was about to argue with him, but he noticed Stubb's face glimmering, slowly lighting up in the dark. The masts blazed again, twice as bright as before.

"God save us!" Stubb shrieked, sinking to his knees.

Now the whole crew bunched together around the main mast, huddling beneath the glinting doubloon and the fire burning in the yardarms.

"Aye men," cried Ahab, stepping amongst us, "study it carefully. The white flame shows us the path to the White Whale. Hand me those rods."

He seized the lightning rods from the deck – in his right hand the link from the mast, in his left the sea chain.

"Hear me, fire," he called defiantly to the masts above. "I've felt your pulse before and still bear the scar."

In the eerie glow I could see the silver streak at the side of his face, twitching as he spoke.

"You cannot destroy me," Ahab howled. "I defy you as a man, and I demand your respect."

Lightning streaks lit up the sky above us and the

flames on the masts doubled in height. But Ahab raged on.

"A man is greater than any lightning bolt," he cried, "greater than any storm or violence sent from nature. You will not consume me. I will blot out your light with my own darkness."

"The boat! Look at your boat, old man," Starbuck shouted.

The harpoon that Perch had forged for Ahab was still lashed to its post in his whaleboat. But the leather cover that protected the blade had been torn off by the wave that crushed the planks. The steel barb was blazing, wrapped in folds of the white fire.

"God is against you," cried Starbuck, gripping Ahab's arm. "Our voyage is cursed, don't you see? Let me rig new sails and steer for home, so we can start a better voyage than this."

Overhearing his words, the terrified crew ran to the bulwarks, ready to climb into the rigging to follow his orders.

"Stay where you are," boomed Ahab. "The first man to touch a rope will feel this point in his belly." He had dropped the lightning rods and snatched his flaming harpoon from the whaleboat. Now he swung it beneath the faces of his crew, herding them away from the bulwarks and towards the main mast.

"You all made an oath to hunt the White Whale," he hissed at us. "You are bound to that oath as much as I am. And if any of you doubt my determination..."

He slowly lifted the burning harpoon blade to his

lips and, with one blast from his cheeks, he extinguished the flame.

Sailors ran in all directions across the decks, in terror at what they'd seen.

For two days and nights we battled against the typhoon. When they weren't working on deck, the crew discussed what had happened to Ahab. His performance had stunned us all, but Flask whispered that it was possible for any man to grip the rods safely, as long as the ship wasn't struck directly by a lightning bolt. Another sailor declared that when the captain's lips had touched the harpoon, he had broken the field of energy that had generated the flames. It was no more than a trick of science, he assured us.

We soon accepted these crude explanations of the strange things we had witnessed.

When we finally cleared the rough weather and the heavy seas, we were approaching the line of the equator that Ahab had been steering for ever since we left snowy Nantucket. We were all nervous, wondering what would happen to us in this lonely stretch of the Pacific.

One day, in the hours before dawn, we were cruising past some rocky outcrops. The night watch was startled by a sound ringing across the waves – high-pitched cries and shrieks. Some of the men said it must be mermaids stretched out on the rocks. But the Manxman, the oldest sailor on the ship, declared that the wild, thrilling sounds we'd heard were the voices of newly drowned men in the sea.

When Ahab came up on deck at first light, he laughed when he heard the story.

"They were seals," he chuckled. "Mothers searching for their lost pups."

An hour later, there was a scream from the rigging, and I saw a man drop a hundred feet from one of the lookout posts, to be swallowed by the sea. He'd just come on watch from his hammock, and must have been too sleepy to keep pace with the rocking of the ship.

Stubb ran to the stern and released the life buoy. This was a hollow cask designed to keep any man overboard afloat until a boat could reach him. But the *Pequod's* life buoy had been hanging too long in the tropical sun. Its boards were parched and shrunken, and the water seeped into it as soon as it landed on the sea. The sinking cask followed our crewmate to the bottom.

"That's what the cries were," said Stubb gravely. "They were a portent of this man's death."

"No," said the Manxman. "They belonged to other men."

Ahab ordered the mates to replace the lost lifebuoy, but all the spare wood was needed to mend the boats damaged by the typhoon. When he heard they were looking for a light cask, Queequeg came to Starbuck and offered the mate his sea chest.

"A life buoy that's a coffin?" choked Starbuck.

"What's wrong with that?" asked Stubb. "We can caulk it so it's watertight."

"Very well," said Starbuck sadly. "I suppose there's nothing else to be done."

He summoned the carpenter and ordered him to nail the coffin shut and caulk the seams. With a shrug, the carpenter carried the box over to a pile of line tubs and balanced it across them.

Ahab was disturbed by the carpenter's hammering and came up from his cabin in a rage. But, when he saw the coffin balanced on the coils of whale line, he only shook his head and went back to his charts.

The Rachel and The Delight

Later that day we sighted a ship, the *Rachel*. She was a large whaler, and she bore down directly on us, her rigging clustered with men.

"She brings bad news," muttered the Manxman. "You'll see."

But, before her captain could call out a word, we heard Ahab shout from the quarterdeck.

"Have you seen the White Whale?"

"Yesterday," came the response. "Have you seen a whaleboat adrift?"

Ahab said he had not, and was calling for his crew to take him across for a gam, when he saw the other captain lowering a boat. In a few minutes he was climbing the boarding nets at our side.

"Where was he?" asked Ahab, as soon as the man had landed on the deck; our captain was almost shaking with excitement. "Is he dead?"

The other captain shook his head. "We were chasing a group of whales when a white hump loomed up out of the waves," he explained breathlessly. "We lowered a fourth boat to go after him, and we think they fastened on with a harpoon.

But they were dragged so far from the ship that we couldn't be certain."

"He escaped, then," whispered Ahab.

"The other three boats were blown in the opposite direction by a squall. I had to pick them up first, of course."

"It was your duty to save the majority," Ahab nodded in agreement.

"By then it was too late to go after the fourth. As darkness fell, we lit a fire in our try pots as a beacon. At first light we sailed to the spot where the men were last sighted, and found nothing."

"Well, thank you for the news," said Ahab coldly. "And I wish you luck with your search." He turned away to return to his cabin.

"You can do more than wish me luck," replied the other man hastily. "My own boy is in that boat. With your ship we can double the area of the trawl. We'll sail five miles apart, sweeping in parallel lines across the ocean, until we find them."

Ahab cleared his throat and stared down at the deck.

"I beg you, Captain Ahab," the other man cried. "Please help me. I have seen you around Nantucket town and hear you are a good man at heart."

But Ahab did not lift his eyes from the planks.

"Then let me charter your ship," the captain offered. "I will pay you, and pay well, if that's the only way you'll help me. Give me your ship for forty-eight hours, Ahab. My son's life might depend on it."

The old Manxman was standing behind me on the

main deck. "You already know what's happened to them," he whispered in my ear. "We heard their drowned spirits, do you remember?"

Up on the quarterdeck, the *Rachel's* master was staring in dismay at his fellow captain. "My son is only twelve years old, sir. I brought him on this voyage to make a man of him, and I will never forgive myself if I lose him to the sea."

Still Ahab was silent.

"I will not leave until you agree to my request," the captain cried in anger. "You have a young son, don't you? I would do the same for you if our positions were reversed. Ah, I think I see you softening, captain, at last. You will help me, after all? I'll call my men to set the sails..."

"Yes, I know you, Captain Gardiner," roared Ahab, "but I do not soften and I will not help you. Already I am wasting time talking with you. God bless you, captain, but I must go. Starbuck," he called to the mate, as Gardiner looked on in shock, "if there are any strangers on my ship in three minutes time, remove them, and sail on as before."

Ahab turned on his ivory leg and left Gardiner alone on the deck. For a moment, the man looked too stunned to move, then he hurried to the side and climbed down to his boat.

For hours we saw his ship tacking across the ocean behind us. But from her restless coursing on the water we could tell she hadn't found her missing boat, or her lost crew.

Ahab was at his mooring hole night and day now. He knew Moby Dick was close by in these waters, and the thought of his tormentor being so near made it impossible for him to rest. He wore a slouching hat and a cape to protect himself from the wind and spray. His meals were brought up to him by the steward, but the captain only picked at his food. The same clothes he wore, that were soaked by rain during the night, were dried where he stood in the morning sun. Since his razors had been melted down to form the harpoon blade, his beard had grown long and gnarled like the roots of an upturned tree. Our captain looked like a wild man, and we moved around him in a glum silence. His only companion was Fedallah, who stood with his arms crossed and his eyes as expressionless as glass. At times I wondered if he was in a deep trance, and I longed to wave a hand across his face to see if he would respond. But I never dared.

Ahab constantly chided the lookouts, ordering them up the masts at the first glimmering of dawn, and nagging them to be vigilant until after twilight. Perhaps he began to suspect they were reluctant to call out a sighting of the dreaded White Whale because, on the fourth day after we met the *Rachel*, he decided he would go up the masts himself.

He tied a knot of ropes together and fixed them to a wooden block. After this had been nailed high on a mast, he ordered Starbuck to hoist him up to this makeshift platform with its rope moorings.

"Perhaps the doubloon will be mine," he taunted the other lookouts, when he'd joined them in the search.

We sailed along the equator, until we sighted another ship on the horizon. It was a whaler named the *Delight* and, when we were close enough to read her name, we could see the shattered hull of a whaleboat suspended in her rigging. The splintered planks had been torn away from the boat's keel, and what remained reminded me of the vulture-pecked ribs of a dead animal — a cage of flimsy bones.

"Have you seen the White Whale?" called Ahab.

"He did this," the other captain answered, pointing at the wreck.

"Did you kill him?" asked Ahab.

"There is no harpoon forged that could do that," replied the other man sadly.

"You are mistaken, captain," yelled Ahab, grabbing the harpoon from his boat and holding it over his head. "I have it here. The blade's been tempered in blood and by lightning, and soon I'll dart it into the White Whale's flesh."

"Then God help you, old man," called the captain.

His ship lurched on a wave and I saw a bulging hammock on the deck next to him. Two sailors were on their hands and knees, sewing its edges together.

"I have only one man to bury," he cried, "out of the five good men I lost yesterday. You sail on their tomb."

I was watching from the main deck with a group

of sailors, and we saw the crew of the other ship lift a plank to the bulwark and place the hammock onto it. As the captain recited a prayer, the sailors tipped the poor corpse into the sea.

"Sail on," boomed Ahab. But he was not quick enough to prevent us from seeing the burial, or from imagining our own.

As we surged away from the other ship, I heard a cry come from her.

"Look, a coffin, lads," shouted a sailor. He had spotted our life buoy hanging above the tiller. "They carry their own coffins on their stern. Leaving our funeral, they sail off to their own."

The Chase Begins

The next day was the clearest I'd ever seen. Sky and sea were the same brilliant powder blue, and hundreds of snow-white birds circled our masts, gliding on a fresh breeze. The sun was a high, golden flame above us, and I felt its heat on my cheeks as soon as I came up on deck. It was a good day to be out on the sea — and a good day to be alive. For the first time in weeks, I saw sailors smiling and joking as they worked. Starbuck was chuckling as he came on duty.

Up on the main mast, strapped to his wood block, Ahab's eyes glowed like coals as he scanned the horizons. His face was wrinkled and chaffed from being out in the elements for so long, and his hair was stained with the dried salt of the ocean spray. But even flint-faced Ahab couldn't resist the charms of this perfect morning. He came down on deck and paced about a bit, and I imagined the thoughts of his family and home slowly melting the icy hate in his heart. He leaned against the bulwarks, sniffing at the breeze and watching the foaming sea. Perhaps he was wondering about his own son. As I watched, I saw him lean forward and shed a tear into the waves.

There was more wealth in that one tiny drop, I thought to myself, than in all the mighty Pacific Ocean.

"Sir," whispered Starbuck, who like me had been studying the captain, "are you well, sir?"

"Oh, Starbuck," said Ahab, turning to face him. "It's a mild wind and a mild-looking sky. It was on a day as beautiful as this that I struck my first whale. I was a boy harpooner, only eighteen years old. That was forty years ago, Starbuck. I've chased the whale for forty years. That's forty years of suffering and storms and peril on the sea. And, in all those years, I've not spent three of them ashore. When I think of my life, of how I've eaten dry crusts when even the poorest landsman has feasted on fresh fruit and fresh bread, how I sailed away from my wife the day after I married her, how I've raged and hated my way around the world in this bloody chase..."

"Captain..." whispered the mate.

"A forty-year fool I am, Starbuck. How am I richer or better than I was, after all these years of killing? The loss of my leg enraged me, drove me on this hunt, but today I feel only old and terribly tired. Stand closer, Starbuck, let me look into a human eye. I see my wife and child in that eye, the green land, the comforts of home. You are a good man, first mate. You will not join us in the whaleboats when the chase begins. I want you safe on the ship, away from Moby Dick."

"But captain," said Starbuck, "you are a noble man

after all. Because there is nothing greater in a man than for him to admit his mistakes or failures. Give up the White Whale. Let's sail away from these waters. I will set the course immediately, and turn the *Pequod* around for home."

Ahab hesitated, his hands resting on Starbuck's shoulders.

"Is it possible?" he muttered to himself. "Could I give up my revenge so easily?"

Then he slowly stepped away from the mate, and his face clouded over until it was as dark as the day the typhoon broke upon us. "Never," he hissed in rage. "I do not know what it is that drives me, goads and lashes me to chase this fiend, but I must see it through.

"But smell that breeze, Starbuck," he went on, his voice soft again. "It smells as sweet as a faraway meadow. They have been making hay, Starbuck, and they are sleeping in the new-mown hay. No matter how hard we work in life, we all sleep at last, and sleep forever. Starbuck..."

But the mate had already left his side, his face grim with despair. Ahab turned back to the sea, and was startled by the reflection of another man staring up at him from the water. It was Fedallah, leaning over the same rail, further along the deck.

That night, Ahab was in his mooring hole when he suddenly thrust out his face and sniffed the sea air like an old bloodhound. "I smell whale," he hissed. Soon a thick, musky scent was drifting across our decks and Ahab ordered that we change course slightly and slacken the sails.

At dawn, we saw a wide slick on the sea, five miles long and smooth as oil.

"His wake," cried Ahab. "All hands on deck."

Daggoo seized a club and began beating the decks. We sailors came running from the forecastle, still dressing as we climbed up to the deck.

"Lookouts," boomed Ahab. "What do you see?"

"Nothing, sir," they replied.

"Take me up there," the captain growled.

Two men hoisted him on his line but, before he had reached his wood-block mooring, we heard him shriek.

"There she blows, a hump like a snow hill. It is Moby Dick."

The other lookouts were all shouting at once, pointing at the whale only a mile ahead.

"Did none of you see him?" Ahab questioned them. "Why didn't you cry out?"

"I saw him an instant after you, captain," said Tashtego from the mast behind Ahab.

"But I was first," said Ahab strangely. "The doubloon is still mine. Only I could have seen him first. Quick, Starbuck," he shouted down to the mate. "He's going to sound. Get the boats ready and bring me down."

As Ahab had commanded, Starbuck and his crew stayed on the ship. From the bulwarks, we watched the other three boats speeding across the water.

The sea grew so calm it was if a sheet had been drawn over the waves. Everything was still except for the rushing boats and the huge, white hump of the whale, lifting and dropping in a ring of green foam. Then, the flock of birds we'd sighted the day before swung out of the sky and landed on the whale's wake, bobbing like shuttlecocks on the ripples he spread with his passage. One of them flapped up over the whale and perched on top of a shattered lance that projected from his hump. All over Moby Dick's body there were scars, gouges and the splintered remains of human weapons, some old, some recent.

"He swims away from us," whispered Starbuck at my side.

"Aye, sir," I replied. "He looks so calm and peaceful, he can't have noticed our boats approaching."

"There are tornadoes hidden in that calm," answered Starbuck.

When our boats were only a few hundred feet from his side, Moby Dick lifted his mighty head and arched forward, showing his broad flukes as he sounded. The three boats were left floating with the birds.

"He'll be down an hour," predicted Ahab. The breeze suddenly blew up and the sea began to swell.

"The birds, captain," cried Tashtego. "Look at the birds."

The white birds were wheeling into the sky and they came streaming down around Ahab's boat. They fluttered around the captain, squawking and snapping their beaks.

Ahab lunged over the side of his boat and stared into the water. In all that blue, he saw a white dot, the size of a butterfly, dancing below him. He rubbed his eyes. The dot grew bigger and suddenly twisted, revealing two long rows of jagged teeth, charging up from the bottom. It was Moby Dick's gaping mouth, yawning beneath the whaleboat like an open-doored marble tomb.

Ahab jumped back and twisted his steering oar sharply in the water.

"Pass me the harpoon," he called to his stunned crew. But, as he yelled, the whale lifted his long jaws out of the water and clamped them around the boat.

Moby Dick was lying on his back like a biting shark, floating just below the boat. His crooked jaw loomed ten feet high, and his teeth cracked and splintered the boat like the teeth of a saw rubbing along a plank, one of them catching in an oar lock and snapping it off, no more than an inch from Ahab's head.

The captain looked up at the clamping jaws, as the whale shook the trapped boat lightly, like a cat shaking a mouse.

Fedallah gazed on without a flicker of surprise. He didn't even uncross his arms. The rest of the crew tumbled over each other trying to get to the far end of the boat.

Ahab was so maddened by the whale toying with him, he took hold of the jaws with his bare hands and tried to force them apart. There was no way he could reach the whale's body with his harpoon, and the other boats were too stunned with shock to row in to help.

But Moby Dick had tired of the game. He closed his great jaws like a pair of shears and sliced the boat in two. As he flipped over and dived, the two ends of the boat floated apart, leaving Ahab and the crew hanging onto the planks, half-submerged in the water.

Now the whale swam swiftly around the castaways, beating the water with his tail. Round and round he went, until Ahab was trapped in the middle of a foaming maelstrom, choking in the spray. Stubb and Flask waited in their boats at its edge, worried that if they approached, the furious whale would rush in and finish off the helpless crew.

Starbuck had not been watching idly. He'd brought the *Pequod* close to the wreck and was about to lower his boat to join the attack.

"Steer on him," Ahab screamed from the ring of foaming water. "Drive him off!"

"Turn the prow," called Starbuck to the man at the tiller, and the ship cut between the whale and his victims. At once the other boats rushed in to pick them up.

When Ahab was dragged into Stubb's boat, he collapsed into an exhausted heap, looking as broken and bruised as a man who has been trampled by herds of elephants. But Ahab was no ordinary man, and he soon rallied, rearing up in the boat and shaking his fist at the distant whale.

"Is my harpoon safe?" he howled.

"Yes, sir," answered Stubb. "I have it here."

"And the men?"

"All accounted for, sir."

"He'll run now," said Ahab, glowering at the whale. "Back to the ship."

When the two boats were lifted and stowed, we rescued the broken parts of Ahab's craft and got ready for the chase. Moby Dick was swimming rapidly towards the setting sun. Even with all our masts covered in sails, it was an effort to keep up with him.

"Sing out when you see him spouting," Ahab called to the lookouts. "And men," he added, turning to the sailors on the main deck. "The gold doubloon is mine because I sighted him first. But I offer it to you again, to the first man that sights him on the day he dies. And if I sight him that fine day, I will pass ten times its worth among you all."

It was getting dark, and Ahab stared out at the fading white shape we were following.

"Get some sleep," he told us. "Tomorrow, we lower for the kill."

The Second Day

At daybreak, the lookouts clambered up the masts.

"Do you see him?" yelled Ahab, before they'd even had a chance to get their footing.

"Nothing, sir," they answered, when they'd made a search.

"He's faster than I thought," growled Ahab. "More sails, Starbuck. Let's make the ship fly after him."

We bowled through the sea, leaving a wide wake behind us.

"The deck's tingling with speed," chuckled Stubb. "The ship's as brave as we are."

"There she blows!" came the cry. "Right ahead."

"You can't escape old Ahab," Stubb shouted into the wind. "We're coming for you, Moby Dick."

Stubb wasn't alone with this bravado. The rest of the crew, including myself, were feeling eager for battle. We'd been chasing this white monster around the world's oceans for months and now, at last, we had a chance to finish the business. Somehow, the failed attack the day before had only made us bolder. Even though the whale had crushed a boat, no sailor had perished and Ahab had been brave enough to fight the whale with his bare hands. How could we fail, with such a fearless captain leading us? All thirty of us in the crew were concentrating on only one thing – death to Moby Dick.

"His spout's vanished, sir," called one of the lookouts.

"It can't have," gasped Ahab. "Look again. Every one of you to the prow."

The whole ship's company climbed into the rigging, or leaned over the bulwarks, scouring the seas for any trace of our prey. Then, bursting out of the waves just off our starboard bow, Moby Dick flaunted his huge, powerful bulk at us as he breached.

A whale can launch his whole body out of the ocean like a dolphin or a shark, and this aquatic gymnastic feat is known as breaching. In the case of a whale, the sheer size of the animal breaking free of the water is enough to take your breath away. Spray flew into the air around him as he cleared the waves, and glittered in the sun like a shower of gem stones. His marble body arched and twisted. Then he hit the surface in a fountain of foaming water.

Again and again he breached, skipping across the sea like a jumping salmon.

"Breach your last, Moby Dick," yelled Ahab. "Your time's almost up. Man the boats."

As soon as the three boats touched the water, I saw Moby Dick change direction and race towards them.

"He's coming for you, sir," Starbuck yelled to Ahab

from the deck. The captain raised himself up in the stern of his boat and studied his enemy.

"Steer for the middle of his head," Ahab ordered the mates, thinking he could approach the advancing whale unnoticed.

But the White Whale was too clever; he swerved to the side and darted into the triangle of boats, striking at their flimsy planks with his tail. The harpooners sank their lances into his side and Moby Dick rolled and twisted, until the three lines were so tied up and tangled they were pulling the boats together. Ahab managed to cut through his line, but the whale corkscrewed in the water so violently that Stubb and Flask could only watch, helpless, as their boats rammed each other. Both boats were holed and broken by the collision.

With the rope ties all snapped or severed, Moby Dick slipped below the surface, leaving the cedar chips of the wrecked boats swirling like grated nutmeg in a swiftly stirred bowl of punch.

Ten men were left screaming in the water, reaching for any flotsam they could find to try and stay afloat. Flask curled his body into a ball around a line tub, trying to lift his dangling legs out of the way of any snapping sharks, while Stubb cried out for help.

"Someone come and ladle me up out of this soup!" he called.

Before Ahab could order his crew to pick up the drowning sailors, his as yet unharmed boat started to rise up out of the sea. The hull shot up fifteen feet into the air. Moby Dick rested the boat and its whimpering crew on his forehead for a few seconds, then sent it spinning into the air and crashing down on the waves.

With the whole hunting party paddling in the sea and all three boats wrecked, the whale turned and swam away, trailing the tangled lines behind him.

Starbuck came to the rescue once more, dropping his boat to pick up the floating crews, oars, tubs and whatever else he could salvage. Back on deck, the men checked their injuries. Some had sprained wrists or ankles. A few were badly bruised. But none of them were fatally wounded.

Ahab was found gripping one end of his smashed boat and, when he was hauled up the side of the

Pequod, the crew saw him hanging from Starbuck's shoulder. His ivory leg had been snapped off, leaving only a sharp, white splinter.

"Aye, lads," sighed Ahab. "He's taken my leg again."

"I can make you another, sir," said the carpenter, stepping forward.

"Never mind that," interrupted Stubb. "Are you wounded, captain? He must have given you quite a kick."

"He can break my bones," joked Ahab, pointing at the shattered peg leg, "but he can't weaken my resolve. Lookouts, which way is he heading?"

"To the north, sir."

"Let's get after him, then. Pile on the sails, Starbuck, and muster the boat crews."

"Can I help you to your cabin, sir?" asked Starbuck, genuinely concerned for his captain.

"No," replied Ahab gruffly, looking all around. "Muster the crews as I said."

"They're all here, sir."

"But I haven't seen him yet. He's not on deck, is he?" Ahab said to Starbuck, his voice fading away.

"Who, sir?" asked the mate.

"Quick, all hands on deck," cried Ahab.

Immediately, we assembled in ranks before our captain. Fedallah was missing.

"It must have been the line that took him," muttered Stubb.

"Silence, man," barked Ahab.

"But, sir," Stubb continued, "I saw him struggling with your tangled line, just before you cut loose. In all the confusion I couldn't be sure, but it must have pulled him under."

"So he's gone," whispered Ahab. "As he prophesied. Will I see him again, though? I hope not."

"Sir?" Starbuck asked him, as the men began asking each other what their captain's mutterings could mean.

"And my own harpoon line did it," Ahab hissed. "But that harpoon sank so deep in the whale's side he'll never pull it out. Even now it must be tormenting him." This thought seemed to lift his spirits. He raised his arms and bellowed like an enraged beast. "Pile on the sails and keep a sharp lookout, lads. Collect the broken oars, mend the boats, sharpen your spare blades. We'll slay him yet, men."

"No, sir," Starbuck protested. "You will never catch him. Twice you've lowered for him. Twice your own boat has been crushed around you. You've lost your leg to the same whale that took it before, and now your evil shadow, Fedallah, has been snatched from you. You've been given so many warnings, captain. We must give up the hunt at once."

"Listen to me, you men," Ahab boomed in a menacing and mighty voice. "Ahab is Ahab and will not be swerved."

Some of the crew cheered when they heard this.

"And when things drown," he continued, "they often rise to the surface twice before they sink. For two days Moby Dick has floated. On the third day I will make him sink, forever. Do you feel brave, men?" he roared.

"As fire," screamed Stubb.

"As lions," yelled the harpooners.

"Then see to my orders," said Ahab. "All night long we'll repair our boats and forge new weapons. When morning comes, we'll be ready for him. Now carpenter, about that new leg..."

Moby Dick

The third day of the chase dawned as fresh and clear as the first. Our lookouts reported no sighting of Moby Dick's spout and, after some hasty calculations, Ahab realized we'd overtaken him during the night.

"Of course," he laughed. "All those harpoons he's towing must be slowing him down. Turn about, Mister Starbuck."

"Now we steer against the wind," said Starbuck gloomily at the tiller, "and towards an open jaw."

"Stand by to hoist me to the mast," called Ahab. "We've got a whale to catch."

An hour passed before the captain's voice woke every sailor. "There she blows. Strong as ever. Make ready to launch."

"Sir, shall I bring you down?" Starbuck called from the deck.

"A moment," Ahab replied. "I'll take a last look at the broad ocean while I can. It hasn't changed since the first time I saw it as a boy, standing on the Nantucket sands. I wish I could know when I'll see it again. But steady, Ahab, don't waver now. We've been sailing all night away from the place where Fedallah drowned. So, I must be safe. Aye, I'll come up here tonight, for a look at Moby Dick's dead body tied to the side of my ship. Lower me, Starbuck. And ready the boats."

For the third time the boats were lowered and the crews worked the oars to pull them away from the side of the ship. The men were thinking of the fight to come and looked around in surprise when Starbuck called from the deck.

"Beware the sharks, lads."

Down in the black water under the *Pequod's* hull there was a seething mass of sharks. They rushed up as soon as the boats were clear of the ship, snapping at the oars and thumping the planks with their tails. After circling all three boats for a few seconds, they clustered around Ahab's boat, so that he was surrounded by dorsal fins slicing through the water.

"They've come for a bite of the whale I'm about to kill," roared Ahab, and there was a cheer from his men.

"I hope you're right, you brave old man," whispered Starbuck, above him on the deck.

The boats hadn't gone far when the whale sounded. The men waited in silence, bracing themselves for the coming fight. A moment later, there was a rumble in the sea below them, a roar that grew louder and louder, until a surge of white water broke to the surface. Moby Dick burst out of it, breaching between the boats, flaunting his huge bulk to his hunters, so they could see the knot of ruined lances and ropes hanging from his flour-white skin.

"Attack!" screamed Ahab. But then his harpoon arm shook with fear as he stared up at the arching leviathan. Roped under the tangle of lines, Fedallah's torn body was pinned tight to the whale's skin. His open eyes fell upon Ahab, and the harpoon fell from the captain's trembling fingers.

"I've seen him again," sobbed Ahab, down on his knees in the boat. "Just as he said. He goes before me, and this prison on the whale must be his hearse. Not made by mortal hands, he said. Oh Ahab, this whale mocks you."

The explosive impact from Moby Dick's breach swamped the two mates in their boats. With a flick of his tail he finished the job, capsizing and crushing them.

Then the whale turned and swam off around the *Pequod*, ignoring the men screaming behind him in the water and Ahab trembling in his still undamaged craft.

"Sir," called Starbuck, who was close enough to make out Ahab's fearful expression, "see how the whale swims away from you. Let him go, I implore you."

"Pick up the men and follow after me," yelled Ahab, struggling to stand and instantly recovering his authority. "Raise the sail," he ordered his crew. "Chase him down."

The whaleboat caught the wind and steered around the prow of the *Pequod*. While Starbuck scooped the men out of the sea, Ahab tore after his enemy.

The sharks that had accompanied Ahab from the beginning of the attack suddenly burst into a frenzy of excitement. They brazenly snapped at the oars, until the wood poles were splintered and cracked.

"Sir," cried one of the rowers, "the blades are getting smaller and smaller."

"They'll last long enough," roared Ahab. "We're almost next to him."

The whaleboat slid into the furrow of water that surrounded the huge, white body of Moby Dick, and lurched as Ahab rushed to the prow with a harpoon. Although the boat was close enough for the crew to prod him with their oars, Moby Dick ignored his harassers and didn't even break his rhythm swimming through the waves. Ahab took this snub as a final insult and, with a vile curse, he raised his arm and sank the harpoon into the animal's body.

Moby Dick writhed sideways, rolling his fin over and smashing it into the whaleboat. Ahab clung to the oarlocks, but three of the rowers were jolted out of their seats and landed in the water. Two of them managed to grab on to the side of the rushing boat and clamber back in, but one man dropped astern, bobbing alone on the ocean.

"Tie that line," yelled Ahab, watching his crew struggling to get a grip on the slippery rope. It flew out of the tub, dragged away by the speeding whale. One of the men managed to loop it around an oar lock but, as soon as it went taught under the huge pressure of the escaping whale, it snapped apart.

Perhaps sensing that he was free again, Moby Dick turned in the water, raised his enormous brow and studied his pursuers. Ahab was cursing and stamping his feet in frustration, but already he was goading his men on to a fresh attack. The *Pequod* was following the captain, her prow to the wind a few hundred yards behind him.

Crashing his jaws together to make a shower of foam, Moby Dick slipped beneath the surface and bore down at full speed upon the advancing ship.

"Look at the whale, sir," screamed one of the

rowers in Ahab's boat. "He makes for the *Pequod.*"

Up on the main deck, Starbuck saw the white flash of Moby Dick picking up speed under the waves. His huge battering-ram head was aiming directly for the starboard bow.

"Will the planks stand it, sir?" whispered Stubb behind him.

"I think not, Mister Stubb," breathed Starbuck. "May God protect us."

The crew had been busy fixing their broken boats and fetching new weapons from the hold, but every man paused to look over the side at the advancing whale. The size of a steam engine, Moby Dick streaked towards them in a white blur.

He hit the ship, and every timber shook. The masts quivered and creaked and, when the *Pequod* yawed

back onto her side from the impact, Starbuck heard water pouring into her hold. Moby Dick swam under them and surfaced on the far side, only a few yards from Ahab in his whaleboat. The whale turned to watch the doomed *Pequod* slowly capsizing under the weight of the flood.

"My ship," cried Ahab. "The second hearse, made of American wood."

The *Pequod's* decks groaned and buckled as she slipped into the water. Some of the men clambered into the rigging, thinking they could outclimb the waves and the mile-deep ocean. Others stood dumbfounded, with the water already lapping around their feet.

"You cursed whale!" screamed Ahab, stepping to the prow with a new harpoon and facing his enemy. "You've taken my ship, but still Ahab hunts you. I'll chase you to the ends of the Earth before I give you up."

With this, he hurled his lance into the whale. Moby Dick reared his head and beat the water with his flukes. He surged away, pulling the line tight behind him and dived. The rope hissed over the wooden groove in the prow, but Ahab saw a coil of it snagged around an oar in the middle of the boat. He leaned down to free it, but Moby Dick was sounding so rapidly the rope jumped up, looped around Ahab's neck and lifted him into the air. The captain shot out of the boat before his crew knew what was happening. Tied forever to his hated whale, Ahab was dragged under the waves and disappeared from sight.

Only the tops of the *Pequod's* masts were visible above the surface of the ocean. The harpooners had climbed to the highest point and were staring at one another in silence as the water bubbled and gurgled around their feet. At last, they were sucked under the waves. The sinking ship created a whirlpool, and everything within a hundred yards of it – men, broken boats, even some of the floating birds – was dragged down behind it. The *Pequod* and her crew finally sank out of sight.

A few birds flew over the churning waters. Soon, the waves were calm and the sea swept over the site of the wreck, rolling on as it has for so many numberless thousands of years.

But there was one survivor of that shipwreck – me, Ishmael. After Fedallah had been lost, Ahab had ordered me into his boat. I was the man who was thrown out into the sea on the last day by Moby Dick's murderous tail, and separated from my fellow sailors. The waves carried me far enough away from the wreck to escape the downward pull of the swirling currents.

As I stared in horror at the open sea and saw the dorsal fins of the sharks rapidly closing on me, a great, black bubble popped up to the surface. It was the coffin, so buoyant that it had broken free from the sinking ship. I clambered aboard, thinking of my lost friend Queequeg and how he had once promised to save my life. For a day and a night, I drifted on the ocean. Then, on the second day, I sighted a sail.

It was the *Rachel*, still cruising the seas searching for her missing crew. I waved to her and she lowered a boat for me — a lost orphan on the ocean, with an incredible tale to tell.

About Herman Melville

Moby Dick might have been his greatest book, but it was also the work that effectively finished Herman Melville's literary career. Contemporary critics hated it. "Not worth the money asked for it, either as a literary work or as a mass of printed paper," was the crushing verdict of one newspaper reviewer. To others, it was too long, garbled, meandering and gloomy. Melville shrugged off the criticism, but the comments must have stung the young author. He had put his heart and soul into the novel, and would live to see it taken out of print and be largely forgotten by the international literary elite.

Melville was born in August 1819, in New York City. His father died a broken man when Herman was only 12. A few years later, the family finances collapsed and he went to sea as a cabin boy. Even as a young man, he had a writer's eye and a mind open to the complexities of the world around him. While his shipmates were off carousing in public bars around the English port of Liverpool, Melville went wandering through the slums, trying to make sense of the inequalities and hardships of the industrial age.

At 21, he was employed on the whaler *Acushnet* and sailed off around the world. The captain was barbaric towards his men, starving and punishing them like a tyrant. So Melville jumped ship in the Marquesas islands in the Pacific, and lived with a tribe of Typee natives for four weeks. When he finally worked his way back to his family home in Massachusetts, he was bursting with stories and tall tales about his adventures. A friend suggested he jot them down for publication.

The result was his first book, *Typee* (published in 1846), describing his experiences among the cannibals. His descriptions of tropical scenes and exotic islanders were a hit with the genteel readers of New England. Melville wasted no time in completing a second South Sea diary, *Omoo* (1847). Reviewers praised the books for their entertainment value as roguish adventures. But if you read them carefully, you will find Melville making real insights into cultural differences, and the corrupting influence of western visitors on local traditions.

With a taste of literary success, Melville married and settled down to the craft of writing. Between 1849 and 1850, he published three novels: *Mardi, Redburn* and *Whitejacket*. These all deal with men or women trying to understand the intricacies of the world, and the dehumanizing effects of money and so-called progress. In 1850, he was at the peak of his powers, and thirstier than ever for knowledge. Melville was reading so much, doctors warned him he might lose his eyesight if he didn't take it easy.

Around this time he met the author Nathaniel Hawthorne (to whom he dedicated *Moby Dick*), and the two men spent hours together, discussing philosophy and politics. The United States was approaching crisis as pressure grew around the issue of slavery. In a decade, the country would break into rival factions and fight a terrible civil war. Melville observed these increasing tensions with anguish. His fears, filtered through the incredibly wide reading he had been doing, resulted in his finest book, *Moby Dick* (1851). Despite the immense strain of completing it, he rushed straight into writing another, *Pierre* (1852). It was to be his last major published work.

In the following years, Melville suffered from depression – his wife's family even tried to convince her he was insane. He also struggled financially. Although he published short stories and gave lecture tours, but never attracted the sam number of readers who had been drawn to his early books. In 1866, Melville was forced to take a job as a customs inspector on the New York docks. He resigned in 1885 and lived quietly until his death in 1891. The only works he published in these later years were small collections of poems which were distributed among close friends.

It was a sad end for such an important writer, though it is possible Melville was content with his sedate life in New York. He had seen more of the world than most people could even dream of, and completed several novels that are still admired today.

Moby Dick is considered by many academics to be the greatest work of prose fiction ever written. It was only because of Melville's refusal to simplify or condense his books to please his audience that he was able to produce this classic. He died in relative obscurity, but he had earned his place in the ranks of the world's finest authors. There can be few greater achievements.

Tales of King Arthur

Retold by Felicity Brooks

A gleaming expanse of water lay before them, with a huge, purple mountain rising up behind it.

Arthur scanned the lake's silvery surface, and without knowing why, he found his eyes coming to rest on a spot in the middle. Without any warning, a hand suddenly shot up from beneath the water, holding a jewel-covered sword and scabbard, which sparkled in the sunlight.

Full of magic, mystery and suspense, these fast-moving tales recount some of the most exciting adventures of King Arthur and the Knights of the Round Table. From the sword in the stone to the last battle, these stories bring to life the characters of Camelot: Merlin the wizard, gallant Sir Lancelot, beautiful Queen Guinevere and evil Morgan le Fay.

FRANKENSTEIN

FROM THE STORY BY MARY SHELLEY

He made his way to the tank and peeped over the rim. There was only the smooth, undisturbed surface of the liquid... Confused thoughts and troubled emotions ran through his mind. He had failed, it was true, but maybe that was for the best. He sighed and relaxed slightly. Then, from the liquid, a huge hand shot out to grab him.

As lightning flashes across the night sky, Victor Frankenstein succeeds in the ultimate scientific experiment – the creation of life. But the being he creates, though intelligent and sensitive, is so huge and hideous that it is rejected by its creator, and by everyone else who meets it. Soon, the lonely, miserable monster turns on Victor and his family, with terrifying and tragic results.

Another Usborne Classic

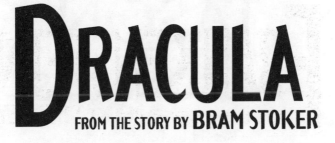

DRACULA
FROM THE STORY BY BRAM STOKER

When the other passengers on the
stagecoach found out where Jonathan
was going, they stared at him in
astonishment. Then they started
whispering in Transylvanian and
Jonathan heard some words that he
knew: *pokol* and *vrolok*. The first word
meant hell, and the second... Jonathan
shivered. It meant vampire.

When Jonathan Harker arrives at creepy Castle
Dracula in Transylvania, he has no idea what to
expect, but all too soon his host's horrible
nocturnal habits have him fearing for his life...
This is the story of a battle against the forces of
evil, as the eccentric Professor Van Helsing and his
brave young friends take on the vilest vampire in
the world.

Another Usborne Classic

JASON & THE ARGONAUTS

Retold by Felicity Brooks

Chiron was still staring at the dancing flames, but his eyes had begun to glaze over as they always did when he was about to see into the future... Then he spoke slowly in a halting, growling voice.

"I see fame and glory... and a long, long journey. I see pain... and tragedy... and a chance to wear a crown."

Jason begged him to explain, but Chiron was already out of his trance... He would say no more.

Deep in the heart of enemy territory, through mountainous seas and uncharted lands, Jason and his fearless crew, the Argonauts, do battle with giants, dragons, monsters and a merciless sea god to bring the legendary Golden Fleece back to Greece.

Another Usborne Classic

Dr Jekyll & Mr Hyde

From the story by
Robert Louis Stevenson

Behind the locked door of Dr. Jekyll's
laboratory lies a mystery his lawyer is
determined to solve. Why does the doctor
spend so much time there? What is the
connection between the respectable
Dr. Jekyll and his visitor, the loathsome
Mr. Hyde? Why has Jekyll changed his will
to Hyde's advantage? And who murdered
Sir Danvers Carew?

This spine-chilling retelling brings Robert Louis
Stevenson's classic horror story to life, and is
guaranteed to thrill and terrify modern readers as
much as when *The Strange Case of Dr. Jekyll and Mr.
Hyde* was first published over a century ago.

Another Usborne Classic

Jane Eyre

FROM THE STORY BY CHARLOTTE BRONTE

Suddenly, a terrible, savage scream
ripped the night apart. It echoed the
length of Thornfield Hall, then died
away, leaving me fixed to the spot.

The scream had come from above
and, sure enough, as I listened, I heard
the sounds of a struggle in an attic
room upstairs. Then a muffled man's
voice shouted: "Help! Help! Help!"

A poor orphan, Jane Eyre is bullied by her rich
relations and sent away to school. Determined to
change her luck, she becomes a governess and
settles happily into a new life at Thornfield Hall.
But why is Mr. Rochester, her employer, so
mysterious, and whose menacing laugh does Jane
keep hearing at night?

Another Usborne Classic

Wuthering Heights

FROM THE STORY BY EMILY BRONTE

...just as I was drifting off to sleep I became aware of a loud, insistent noise. Somewhere outside, a branch was knocking against the window, scratching and thumping in time to the wailing of the wind.

Eventually I could bear it no longer. I climbed out of bed, determined to break off the branch and put an end to the noise... but instead my fingers closed on a small, ice-cold hand!

High on the windswept Yorkshire moors, an old farmhouse hides dark secrets. What is the starnge history of Wuthering Heights? Why has Heathcliff, his mysterious owner, cut himself off from the world, and who is the unearthly girl wandering the moors at night? The answers bring to light a passionate tale of two generations torn apart by love and revenge.

Another Usborne Classic

VICTORIAN GHOST STORIES

We listened intently. The sound changed
to little pants and fierce sobs, getting
closer and closer, as though a person in
distress were walking to where we were.

"There's a child out there!" Simson
whispered urgently. "What's a child
doing out so late?"

I remained silent. I knew that it
wasn't a child, not a living one anyway.

Seven spine-tingling stories have been dug up from
the grave and dusted down for this classic selection
of hauntings, howlings and horrors. Enter the world
of ghouls and ghostly apparitions, as the dead return
to torment the living.